WHO IS JOE DANIELS?

DOES IT MATTER?

Remembering our roots

By

Geoff Miller

Copyright © Geoff Miller 2024
This book is sold subject to the condition that it shall not, by way of trade or otherwise, be lent, resold, hired out, or otherwise circulated without the publisher's prior consent in any form of binding or cover other than that in which it is published and without a similar condition including this condition being imposed on the subsequent publisher.
The moral right of Geoff Miller has been asserted.
ISBN: 9798340827968

*To Flip, that you may know a little better
(and then not forget) where you came from,
and to Cheryl, Mandy, Karl, Dean, Jordan and Catherine
that you don't forget.*

Time present and time past

Are both perhaps present in time future

And time future contained in time past

T.S. Eliot

Burnt Norton, The Four Quartets

CONTENTS

ACKNOWLEDGEMENTS i
CHAPTER 1 1
CHAPTER 2 11
CHAPTER 3 23
CHAPTER 4 31
CHAPTER 5 48
CHAPTER 6 58
CHAPTER 7 72
CHAPTER 8 80
CHAPTER 9 89
CHAPTER 10 97
CHAPTER 11 106
CHAPTER 12 112
CHAPTER 13 118
CHAPTER 14 128
CHAPTER 15 132
ABOUT THE AUTHOR 135

ACKNOWLEDGEMENTS

This story wasn't really initially written for a wide readership but it is a joy to share. Inspired by an off-the-cuff comment, it was written to fulfil its dedication: to help a batch of grandchildren find out about and remember their roots. Other families will have their own stories to tell and all stories are valid.

What you read here is mostly true though I have judiciously changed a few names here and there. But it has relied much on fickle memory and, like all told stories, reflects the teller's redaction. Mistakes are all mine, so are omissions and exaggerations. Remember, Geoff always liked the dramatic.

Thanks go to Gary – we are the last ones standing, Gaz – and of course to Elaine who has heard it all before, (too?) many times. She has kept patience and even managed to encourage. To Richard, my second oldest pal (I'm afraid you can't compete with that bath-time in the sink), thanks for yet again checking the comprehensive school lad's grammar. Some educational failings last a lifetime, but you already know that.

Finally, to those to whom it is dedicated, never forget our story. Never be restricted by it, too. It has played its part in creating you but it should not totally define you. Not if you are prepared to ask questions and take some Miller feistiness into an unchartered future. That future is yours, at least for now. Go well.

Geoff Miller

Hal and Vee, Billingham, 1986

Mary Ellen and Pa at Pontin's Holiday Camp, 1964

CHAPTER 1

Where does a story begin, or end, for that matter? I suppose it depends on the story you are wanting to tell, though I would contend that no story has a true beginning or an end. Of course, new chapters emerge, there are new people, significant events (often more significant in retrospect), just as there are closings, finishing moments, and times to pause before moving on. In reality, these are merely the foundations for the next episode, just like they rely on previous events to help weave the thread that you follow. I suppose most stories when told begin with something: a birth or meeting (however accidental) or a 'happening' like a war or a leaving. Something that nudges the memory, helps the recall, sets something in motion like a domino crashing into its neighbour or a chess move that reconfigures the board. Events, no matter how seemingly co-incidental, help anchor and ground the tale being told or at least offer a marker, a starting block, for a beginning – or an end, for that matter.

My story struggles to find a beginning. Perhaps it started in Russia or Poland, Belfast or Manchester. Each of these places play their part and could make a case for themselves. Perhaps it started with a falling in love or a desire to escape the clutches of a sad but powerful matriarch? Like all stories, it has manifold events as well as many mysteries, but there again, so does all life. In truth, what went before is lost, at least for now, and the ending – well, that still has to be written. But even incomplete stories can still be told. This episode – for it is just a passing moment, but it is mine, and that pleases the ego – or set of episodes, begins with a birth. A rather ordinary one at that. A young couple recently liberated from the clutches of a domineering mother, an empress who ran the family firm, are given a council flat on the fast-developing outer housing estate close to the airport in Manchester. And then off we go, like the first turn of a helter-skelter ride.

Wythenshawe was no doubt inspired by post-war manic home building. The empty land south of the city provided the perfect landscape for what we would now probably call a new town, but then it was a mere extension of the city built for families from the slums of the centre of Manchester: Moss Side, Levenshulme, Hulme and the like. Apparently, these young war couples could be flung to far places in all directions: Hyde or Heywood, Audenshaw or Warrington. In this case, Wythenshawe. Prior to the building of the sprawling housing estate, Wythenshawe was probably best known for its park and great hall. A sister to Tatton Hall some miles away in Cheshire, it is a black and white Tudor building which was surrounded by 250 acres of verdant landscape, formal gardens, stables and tennis courts. Exciting stories of its past abound. Robert Tatton, defending his Royalist roots yet overwhelmed by Roundheads in the Civil War, was perhaps the one person who most filled the imagination of young council estate kids. The Tatton family survived living in the hall (following a £700 fine paid to the Roundheads) and, by

1926, the house and land were bequeathed by its then owner Earnest Simon (First Baron Simon of Wythenshawe) to Manchester City Council. For the socialist republic of Manchester, it was the siting of their grand 'garden city' project. The first houses in Benchill had been built before the Second World War but most came afterward. Then development followed development – sunshine houses by the dozen, all in neat rows, with gardens and indoor toilets. By the late 1950s, almost 100,000 people lived on what was by then the largest housing estate in Europe. Sadly, that was not to be its only claim to fame. People flocked to this old agricultural land, now covered in cement and bricks and promising a utopia for the working classes. There were still odd bits of farm land, pigs and cows, a few schools and churches, and even fewer shops and amenities. But they were all promised for the future. Unfortunately, the project soured so that by 2007, the *New York Times* described the estate as an 'extreme pocket of social deprivation and alienation'. But that is to get ahead of ourselves, for stories take time and time is counted in lives lived.

For Hal and Vee Miller in the 1950s, this potted history was of no account whatsoever. Freedom beckoned: green fields, inside toilets, young neighbours chasing similar dreams and, most of all, their own place to live, their own door to shut, and leaving behind not just the slums but the matriarch 15 miles away back in Moss Side. Added to that, she, the matriarch, was terrified of the sound of the planes as they flew into and out of nearby Ringway Airport, so much so that she ducked and covered her head for each one. Much to the delight of her son and his young wife it was a grateful addition to the reasons she would rarely visit!

Hal and Vee were a classic wartime couple, if not a bit on the young side. Courting was by and large limited to visits to the local fleapit cinema. There, Hollywood dreams filled fantasies while back row fumbling satisfied more immediate desires. Hal thought of himself as a local wide boy and though small, he could strut his stuff with a swagger. He earned his spending money mainly at Proctor's Boxing Gym where, for a coin or two, he would spar with would-be greats. Even the odd champion, he told us. For a time, he was sure he would make professional until one night at a large amateur bout he was told to 'throw the fight' to an upcoming lad. He did a good job of it, and paid with bruises to his face and his battered ego. Never again, he declared; he had no desire to become someone else's punchbag and end up like the old punch-drunk guys who spent their days in the Great Western on the High Street. He turned his attention to a plethora of ruses: a sometime chimney sweep, a window cleaner, a small shop dealer selling horsemeat (not fit for human consumption), and the odd labouring job here and there.

As a young lad, Hal's greatest love was his time in Yorkshire staying with his Aunt Saranne in Deneby, and labouring at its pit which worked the old Barnsley seam. Tales abounded of his time in the pit: the delicacies of lard sandwiches to settle the dust, the drinking games and the contests of strength. His uncle's greatest party trick was to let his wife dance on his chest in her stiletto heels, or so Hal claimed. Like many other boy miners, his job was to turn the coal-loaded carts on to the next track. With their heavy loads, they came fast, and one slow move on a lad's part could cost an arm. He loved the wet and the dark but most of all the comradery. No doubt, for a young lad from the big city, it was an adventure and one he could brag about. However, Vee, his girlfriend at the time, hated the Yorkshire small town experience. She couldn't stand the washing lines draped across the front street of the back-to-back houses. She was offended by the miners' only bus routes, which meant you had to walk miles to get home from the cinema. She wasn't keen on staying at home with the women while Hal was acting big with the men in the clubs.

Vee (really Vera, but Vee was enough) was the youngest of six girls (not counting miscarriages and infant deaths) and she had two younger brothers. Her army veteran dad was a tough old boot who suffered with his chest, and suffered fools even less. Hard days of work as a boilerman invariably finished with his head over a steaming bowl covered in a towel. Chlorine gas was the nasty enemy he had met in the war. He could be rigid and inflexible, refusing to attend one daughter's wedding because she had become a left footer with Father Riff Raff's lot in order to marry her GI boyfriend. Yet he was no churchman himself. On the other hand, he had a good Mancunian sense of humour. Hal often recounted the night he called to take Vee out to the pictures. She's busy, he was told, with her house chores. However, if it was a picture he really wanted to see, rather than waste the tickets he could take one of her younger brothers, Bill or John. They could easily recount the story later to Vee. Hal was not impressed. Vee's mum was universally known as Granny Mac. Tall and slim, she baked wonderful cakes, favoured her boys with a full sausage while the working girls managed with half. She cleaned (a common family trade) at the local public house, which was a good thing because she liked her stout and could bring a jug home with her. She was a saintly sort who aimed to keep the peace, liked her grapes peeled, and was known to her grandchildren for threepenny pieces and Kit Kats.

Hal's fearsome mother was not known for handing over any cash; rather the opposite, though she had a ready source of Blue Ribands which she would dispense if you met her demands. They were tucked away, hidden in her dark, secret parlour next to the scullery. Perhaps with only the pictures and Yorkshire visits to amuse her, it was inevitable that Vee succumbed to pregnancy. It didn't cause too much of a storm – well, perhaps it did, but she weathered it. Those later war years were quite accustomed to such events. The trajectory was, however, usually pretty straightforward to follow, even if it involved little choice. Hal and Vee were married in the local church, not one they often frequented but at least, for her dad's sake, it was Protestant, or to be precise, Low Church. Vee had not long passed her sixteenth birthday while Hal was almost a whole year older, if not wiser. There was no time or money for anything fancy, but Vee managed a new smart grey suit with ruby coloured trimmings and they spent the afternoon at the pictures. The day was, however, not without its drama.

Like all good grooms, Hal arrived at the church early, which proved to be a good move. Mary Ellen, his manipulative mother, had beaten him to the vicar. She knew the vicar, of course, because she was clever enough to cross palms with silver when it came to people she thought might be useful, 'paying forward' as she called it. But beware those whose open hands received her generous donations for she would at some point call in the debt. Such a survival practice was in her bones and she was, for a small-time player, quite adept. She had got young John, Hal's brother, to ask the vicar to visit her. Why waste energy walking round to the vicarage when you were the one giving the donation? Anyway, she was not built for exercise. Hal reckoned she probably cried a little, in search of some sympathy, and maybe even pulled off one of her infamous fainting tricks, usually done with a loud and staggering sigh. Hal could give you a wonderful impression because he had seen it so often. Then, he mused about the meeting with the vicar. He imagined her falling back into her chair just next to the fire before eventually getting to the point. She hated revealing secrets, but she was in a corner, so needs must.

Family secrets are fascinating things. How is it that the people we know most intimately can also be the ones who carry the deepest of secrets? We often talk about the desire to live authentic lives, being true to ourselves, even being out and proud, but in reality, we find those closest to us the hardest ones with which to bare our souls. Perhaps in some strange way we all need that bit of us that is only ours or perhaps we find it hardest to bear our shame to those we know best. But family secrets are often the juiciest, at least to the distant observer. The intrigue wets a vicious curiosity no matter how absurdly unimportant or how deeply hurtful its revelation sets in train. Without them, where would authors be? Just how many stories would be written? And of course, secrets told like this usually breed. They are rarely resolved blips, much more likely to be just the next instalment of the family soap opera. Secrets are, after all, the proud parents of most dynasty dramas. In Mary Ellen's case, she couldn't cope with revealing any sign of weakness unless it could be easily contained with a shudder and a mock fainting fit. Usually, her lips were sealed and one way or another she sealed everyone else's. No one will know exactly what she told the vicar, for only he and she would be harbingers of the detail, but she must have spun at least a tale that would place him in an impossible position. Hopefully, for his sake, before she played her card, he had a sizeable donation in his inside pocket.

As Hal was taken aside into the musty vestry moments before his bride was due to arrive, the vicar realised that he could procrastinate no longer. He knew his next actions may jeopardise future donations from Mary Ellen, but any other action would be worse than her intimidation. It could make him open not merely to accusations of weakness (of which on any account he would find it difficult to acquit himself) but would sail close to an illegality of some sort. He couldn't be sure when the secret would get out, but his only bit of wisdom was to know that secrets like this almost always do. To be fair, perjury was not his preferred *modus operandi*. He, the vicar, didn't really know how to play it, but he had given it some thought. He showed the young lad the details he had prepared to put in the landscape green registers which he would also copy onto the Marriage Certificate.

'I'm afraid you might be a bit shocked by this, Mr Miller,' he muttered, preparing the ground as best he could. Hal didn't get very far before he noticed the bombshell these notes contained. At first Hal thought the vicar had made some stupid mistake, then his fist clenched at the possibility he had to defend his honour to some stranger. Only then did he read more carefully the box on the form that contained the groom's name: *Maurice Daniels*, then in brackets underneath *(known as Harold Miller)*; the next one, entitled groom's father, read *Joe Daniels*.

'Who is Maurice Daniels?' he declared.

'You are, Mr Miller.'

'Who the hell is Joe Daniels?'

'I think he is your father, at least according to the Birth Certificate your mother showed me last week. But for any other details, I'm afraid you will have to ask her.'

At that point, they were told the bride had arrived. Hal was stunned into silence, a rare thing, but the cat was out of the bag and it wasn't going back. It was soon to be in black registrar's ink, too. No one could tell how this testosterone-filled lad would react. His fists stood clenched but firmly at his side. The wedding went ahead. He would deal with this later he explained to his perplexed pretty bride. Afterwards, they went straight to the picture house though neither could remember which film was showing. For Hal, it was *Joe Daniels* who dominated his brain and Mary Ellen who had the heat of his fury. Vee, in her usual manner, calmed him and brought him round to some perspective. At least they were together. She, of course, had some worries of her own. Later that day, she packed an old battered case and moved from the terraced house in Talbot Street to the large, overbearing, house in Heywood Street. She could smell its musty old-lady scent long before the door opened to let her in.

CHAPTER 2

By any measure, Mary Ellen's was a big house but that only added to its overbearing shadow for a young pregnant girl. Decorated in Victorian browns and greens, it was dark and dingy and smelt of pee-pot, Soir de Paris and old lady. It was also a full house. Mary Ellen ruled the roost from her throne in the corner at the fireside. She managed the kettle, which was on a metal swing contraption so that it could be placed right over the fire and then pulled back for Mary Ellen to spit on its base and check the heat. Next to her was a table covered in a piece of dark green oil cloth and upon which was a large tea pot and some 'builders' mugs'. This was the epicentre, the control room of her empire, and she could do all that was necessary with little more than a swivel of her ample hips. Here, she drank large gulps of tea; here, she doled out her magnanimous loans and collected her interest-laden dues; and here, best of all, counted her coins. Everything was recorded in her little book before she eventually scurried it away to her lair in the room next door. She shared the middle room as a bedroom with Pa, her beleaguered, belittled husband. Vee's dad was not impressed with him. Henpecked was too kind a term. But then he wasn't the one who had to share a bed with the larger-than-life old woman. Maybe he was still lured by the smell of Soir de Paris, but I doubt it. True, she had probably been attractive once. It was a good job he had a long memory. Now he was just useful, the matriarch's personal valet: bring this, Pa; fetch that, Pa; tie my shoelaces, Pa, I get dizzy when I bend over! He was a gentle man who preferred a quiet life, glad of the odd pint and a pipe of tobacco. Then there were the three lads. Hal, the eldest, had a room in the attic, the room he would now share with his bride; the youngest was light-fingered John (always ready to help himself to something). He was an expert scammer long before computers and the internet had become universal. *Think of a pitiful situation and use it to make a little on the side* might have been his personal motto. 'Mind that was a terrible tram crash yesterday, pity those poor children,' he told the punters at the Great Western Pub. 'I'll organise a whip round myself just to help out.' He wouldn't be seen in the Great Western for a good while, so hopefully no questions would be asked and no one was any the wiser as to the safe delivery of the cash collected. And the accident-struck family would not be any better off. Finally, there was the favourite, the middle son, Walter, (named after Pa) who basked in the oedipal sunshine of Mary Ellen. It's unusual for the middle son to be the favourite, but he had the position firmly taped. Though perhaps he wasn't really the middle one if you count Hal as an earlier mistake. Like Pa, Walter would do Mary Ellen's bidding, act as the broker, dance to the tune or be the agent, but unlike Pa he did not remain silent. He actively took her side, mincing with sickening regularity. For all this, he was rewarded with saliva-full kisses, embarrassing cringe-worthy expressions, maternal affection, and cash, probably under the table. Fortunately, he was physically weak, hated violence and afraid of his elder half-brother. So, he proved a dangerous but easily controlled nemesis.

As if that wasn't enough, there were others, too. Slobbering Mrs Humber was ensconced in what was once the parlour. She was the widow of the local bible-basher, forced to take a room in Mary Ellen's empire as her income diminished. She rarely left her room except to empty the pee-pot she kept under the bed, which provided an inviting earthy aroma to all her infrequent guests. She at least provided a kindly front to Mary Ellen's other enterprises and she paid rent to boot. Another rent-paying lodger was Tommy Rand. He was orphaned at a young age and was brought up in the children's home in Styal, next to the infamous women's prison. His personal hygiene left much to be desired, from his long dirt-ingrained finger nails to nicotine-ingrained clothes. Yet he had one great skill at his fingertips: he could bake cakes and, wow, could he ice them. Intricate filigree of icing covered each masterpiece, worthy of any wedding feast, especially if you took no notice of the fingernails. It earned him a living, and a good one at that, and with no dependants, he could spread the dosh. Last but never least, the most loved of all was Papa, Pa's aged dad. Almost toothless but as hard as nails. He had walked to Manchester from Yorkshire during the Great Depression carrying a grandchild. He hardly knew the way, so he followed the railway tracks. He put his head down and kept his own counsel: "See all, hear all, say nought." He liked strong, blue, very smelly cheese which he kept in a tin along with maggots. He would light his pipe and open a bottle of stout to pour over the cheese. When the maggots surfaced, he would cut a wedge and pull the maggots out before enjoying the mature taste! He always had a soft spot for the young ones, and Vee became his favourite in no time. She was rewarded with bits of extra sugar or butter and the occasional square of chocolate. Ration books were still very much in use. It was a small but welcome positive glimmer in her early married life. It was into this cosy little community that Vee brought her pathetically few belongings and here she submitted herself to the rule of Mary Ellen, the unrelenting Mother Superior.

From school, Vee worked with her eldest sister in a green grocer's in Sale. Dolly, her sister, was the manageress, and it was a reserved occupation. Vee had been lodging with her aunt but once she was married and "beginning to show", it was too far to travel each day, though she continued for a short while. She was quickly and efficiently inducted into the Miller household. Friday evening was the ritual of the weekly reckoning. Everyone handed over their pay packets to Mary Ellen and received their pocket money for the week to come. Not so much to spend frivolously, but for bus fares and the odd bit of bait money. It wasn't so strange to Vee: she had handed over her pay packet to her mum in Talbot Street, but she would admit to a little resentment about doing the same to Mary Ellen. It was different for Hal. Somehow, he had kept his calm after the wedding day bombshell, though in truth he was inwardly still reeling from the can of worms opened in the musty vestry at St Margaret's Church. Mary Ellen would have preferred to carry on as normal, continuing to ignore the event, enjoying the one extra pay packet, at least until the baby arrived. Hal chose to quietly confront the old woman which, for him, was quite tactful. It didn't work. She shuddered and fell into her chair with a long stuttering groan. 'Pa, get me my salts,' she cried. 'Best to let sleeping dogs lie,' she told him. 'Least said the better,' she announced, as if he had some cheek to demand answers to any questions. And then she firmly clamped her lips; it was the end of the matter, at least as far as she was concerned. He had lost the battle if not yet the war. What Hal now knew for definite was that Pa was not his real father and that the mysterious Joe Daniels was. He felt no bitterness towards Pa, though he harboured some kind of contempt that yet again Pa had submitted to her dominance. But the real puzzle he would like to solve was, *Who was (or perhaps is) Joe Daniels?* What was clear was that Mary Ellen was not going to give any secrets away; she would not reveal any of the mystery. He was annoyed at the deceit, intrigued and unnerved by the mystery it posed, and felt slightly off-balance in his own skin. He determined to seek his revenge, to break the silence, but for now it was his young bride and the fast approaching birth of their child that distracted and calmed him somewhat. A faint memory emerged of him as a baby and a long-bearded man with a dark coat and strange hat taking him away in a pram, a policeman returning him to the claustrophobic flabby arms of a slobbering Mary Ellen. But he could make no more sense of it. It was a mystery that would prove to be a lifelong regret, a constant niggle that never resolved itself, though in time there were a few more hints and clues and rumours ... always rumours.

For those of us who take for granted who our birth parents are, it is hard to understand what the not knowing might feel like. For Hal, it started with a little niggle, easily brushed off and buried for a while. But the not knowing simmered. There was a gap, an empty part, a missing piece. It was not helped by his turbulent relationship with Mary Ellen. She was his mother right enough, but he would always be the one who stood up to her wiles, and he usually paid the price. He never spoke much about his birth conundrum, but like all suppressed anger and disappointment, it raised itself in a general disquiet that could appear left field. Occasionally he would dream fancifully of who his real father might have been and whether knowing him would have filled the gap, replaced the metaphoric missing limb or, indeed, whether it would have just raised further questions. But for the most part, his concern remained buried deep.

Up in the attic, an alternative power centre in Heywood Street began to emerge. Hal began his plan of attack, his bid for liberation, though for all intent and purpose life carried on as Vee grew round with child. She, too, soon got the hang of how to manage. She knew the girls in the wash-house well, which was both a blessing and a laugh in a dreary week. She regularly walked round to see her mum and her sisters, and to spoil her little brothers. The shame of pregnancy slowly lifted as she became a married woman of just sixteen. Back in Heywood Street, she learned how to dodge Mary Ellen and to charm the others, especially Papa. To her life-long disappointment, she had never learned to bake the bread and cakes that her mother produced each Monday, but she picked up a few culinary skills here and there as she dreamed one day of her own kitchen. When things felt really low, she mused on the words of her distraught father as he found out the news of the embryonic baby growing in her womb: 'Well girl, you have made your bed. Now you will have to lie on it.'

There was nothing original, or for that matter particularly kind, in this over-used adage of exasperation, but she learned how to spin it to her advantage. It was her bed and she would lie in it. That hint of rebellious determination reared its head – she would need it in the years to come. Above all, she would get on with it, whatever it was. Of course, she, at least, had Hal, strong, dashing Hal with his square chin and mop of black hair. Together against the world, well against Mary Ellen.

Hal inducted Vee into the rules of the game. Pulling back the rug in their bedroom, he lifted a floorboard and retrieved a small wooden box. Unlocked, it revealed cash, notes and coins carefully laid out. 'In here we put any spare cash we can get our hands on,' he told her. 'For our future, no one else's,' he said. 'Where do you get it from?' Vee mused. 'Anywhere,' he said and soon she learned what that meant. The odd boxing bout, tips from window cleaning or sweeping chimneys, and many other ruses. Basically, as much money as he could not declare to the dragon downstairs. 'Never tell her the full story,' he told Vee. 'Wherever you can, underestimate your wages, any tips or gifts. Give them to me or put them straight in here. Above all, keep mum, tell nobody.' He had certainly picked up some of her traits, or maybe they were already in the gene pool that Joe Daniels had bestowed.

Hal liked to count his money in secret. Making secret

stashes became a life-long habit. Of course, Vee knew what he was doing, though he would sometimes hide it from her, too. It was a transferable skill that she also learned and, on occasions, was the saving grace of her family. Usually, he got his money the hard-earned way, but occasionally he would, to Vee's disapproval, stoop a little lower. Rarely, but definitely on occasion, there were trips to the pawn shop on Princess Street where, under the shadow of the three balls, he would trade in items he had pilfered from the house. He was careful and, in his own way, thoughtful. He limited it to the occasional lapses that Mary Ellen made, her poor keeping of any inventory, never from the lodgers or Papa. A memorable occasion was when he raided the blanket box and another the cutlery drawer. Vee soon found her own ways of more respectably adding to the coffers.

Hal was always a would-be entrepreneur, a would-be small-time businessman. Until the day he died, he harboured the dream of owning a newsagent and tobacconist. Though perhaps he never faced the truth – that he would probably have smoked the profits. He was never really much of a drinker (rum was his tipple of choice), but cigarettes proved to be a greater downfall. He began smoking young (perhaps twelve or thirteen). Back then, you could get two cigarettes and a few matches from a vending machine. Later, he easily progressed to Capstan's Full Strength and later in life the orange cigarette box competed with his fingers for the same lurid colour. He took up a variety of jobs, the odd labouring shift, the selling of meat – horse meat, to be precise, but never to be admitted. Perhaps he excelled at setting up his own window cleaning round and chimney sweep business. It went well and the complex brushes for the chimneys' cleaning proved a good investment. It went so well that Mary Ellen coveted its potential. She took over the bookkeeping and set Walter and John up as hands-on help. Yet again, his independence was easily thwarted and yet again she out-manoeuvred him to rule the roost. It soon became part of her empire.

The baby's arrival made any grand gestures towards freedom impossible. Linda was born in the August – a tiny and soon to be feisty little doll. She soon won hearts and made her mark. Hal simmered but was blighted by a burst appendix which put him out of action for a while and would become more than a thorn in the flesh for years to come. Still, for Vee, it made sure he avoided conscription and even National Service. Meanwhile, she found a job that pleased her. She had always been a good swimmer. Well, perhaps not always; she had found (or was it lost?) her feet when bragging to her school friends that she could swim as she walked along the pool floor, making what she thought were the right arm movements. She was quickly moved to the deep end where she had no option but to swim or sink. Soon she became the school's champion swimmer. She won cups that were proudly displayed in the school entrance foyer and helped her avoid more taxing tasks. Now that very same skill came to her rescue. A private swimming pool in the town needed a lifeguard who could give swimming lessons. She was in her element and as it was a job reasonably well paid, with some tips and the odd extra lesson allowing her to contribute to the box secreted under the floorboards. It's hard to remember that they were barely more than children themselves. Useful to Mary Ellen as wage slaves and extra ration books, nevertheless they too breathed the post-war euphoria that promised a better future for their kind. Their dreams were, by any standard modest, a job with reasonable pay, pay that didn't have to be handed over in return for a pittance of infantilising pocket money, a front door that was theirs and the chance to live their own way, no matter how naïve or foolish. However, escape from the clutches of Mary Ellen and Heywood Street needed a breakout plan more akin to Colditz. Too many obstacles made it seem impossible, but post-war change was in the air. Change that brought with it just a glimmer of hope. For this young couple, this came in the form of the local council elections.

The Labour and Co-operative Society had long governed Manchester, at least in recent memory. It should have been the natural home of Hal: his Yorkshire mining family, his hard graft to make some kind of living, his yearning for his own place, his dream of a better future. All the hallmarks of a labour activist or voter at least. But Hal and Vee were desperate and focused. As the loudspeaker-topped cars drove around Moss Side declaring this or that, touting for a vote, they also made promises. Evelyn Hill belonged to an old Conservative family and was equally desperate to keep her family dynasty in the game. It was by chance that it was her surgery they attended. Indeed, it was probably a mistake, but Hal had no qualms about using an opportunity to his advantage.

'It's like this, Councillor, quite simple really. You get us a place to live, away from here, in one of those new estates. Then you can use us as an example for your campaign and we will vote for you.'

He meant it and she did it. Exactly one week later, they were offered a flat, twelve miles away in the fast-growing council development of Wythenshawe. Vee was deliriously happy. The only problem was telling Mary Ellen. Oh, and Hal getting a regular job!

It was a sombre evening when, with a smirk, Hal told Mary Ellen. He let her get the false faint and the cry of pity out of the way. It was a dramatic scene: Pa scurrying to get the smelling salts, Walter trying to make some sweet tea, Tommy Rand looking awkwardly into the yard, and John doing a quick bunk to the lav. Even Mrs Humber popped out of her room to check what was happening. Vee stood crying, but Hal was prepared, standing firm as a boxing punch bag, reeling slightly but going nowhere. *This time*, he thought, *this time*. She soon recovered her decorum and realised she needed a different strategy to keep them under her roof and under control.

'You don't know how lucky you are here! You are both far too young to make it on your own. You have no furniture, no money. You will have to get a job. You'll soon be running back here. Save yourself a lot of trouble. Go upstairs, have a talk, and think about what you are doing.'

She looked at his reaction and thought she needed to finish the job by playing her ace card. 'By the way, Hal, I had Lillian [Walter's girlfriend] do a little spring-cleaning upstairs today. That squeaky floorboard under your bed was an easy giveaway. I've put all the contents of that box in a safe place. You could have some of it to take Vee and the little girl out for a nice day at the seaside.'

'We just want our own home!' cried Vee, wishing it was all over and feeling it *was* over. Mary Ellen had them trapped in her clutches again. Hal was not phased. He kept his cool.

'Well, you can keep the money. There wasn't much there after all. Just so you know, I start on the buses next week. We'll move out at the weekend.'

Stunned silence, cue another faint.

'Vee, you go and pack, I'll get Linda. We are staying at Vee's mam's for a few days and her sisters are already working hard to help us sort out the flat. We won't have everything, but we will manage.'

*

He carried the dainty little girl up to the attic. She was somewhat bewildered and thought bedtime had come far too early.

'But how will we manage without the money-box?' Vee cried to him in the attic room.

'I'd already rumbled that,' he said, 'and moved the money. I wondered why Lillian was snooping around. I just left enough for them to think they had made a find. Call it rent!'

'Well, are there any more secrets?' Vee whispered as she went in for a relieved cuddle, 'because I have one to tell you. Best you know now ... I'm three months gone.'

CHAPTER 3

Flat six, Darnbrooke Drive, was no luxury mansion. But it had a bathroom, a kitchen and a front door! The small, but swelling, family moved south to Wythenshawe without much fuss but with great relief. There they joined a developing community of refugees from the city slums. The vast majority were young families and Vee was surprised at how many she knew. She called a lot of the women by their maiden names. She knew them from school, the washhouse, the dance floor at the Ritz and the queues for the pictures. Vee's sisters did her proud by collecting together enough essentials to set up a home, and the money Hal had secreted away came in useful. It was all pretty sparse but they would manage without fancy lampshades, matching kitchen stuff, or bedroom eiderdowns for that matter. Mary Ellen accepted the move without much grace but for now she let it happen without reacting. No further ado, so to speak.

The flats were quite new; young families lived on each landing, which smelled of food. At least you knew what was cooking for tea, though it all merged into some school-like canteen aroma, the cabbage easily dominating. Quickly, new friendships were forged, some which would last a lifetime. The Barratts lived on the same floor: May and George with their children Alma and John, both slightly older than Linda and her developing embryo. Above them were the

Mushinskis, a Polish family, friendly and great neighbours except for the smell of garlic which often fought with cabbage for dominance. Hal hated it though in later life loved it in a stew as long as he never knew that it was the magic ingredient. Life was marked with parties and fun, and Vee was in her element. The birth of Brian was a delight and this time Vee felt it was very much her baby and her family. Her new-found friends rallied around her and she was never short of a friendly cup of tea or some words of wisdom from one of the slightly older and more experienced mothers. She was growing up and the family was, too.

Few Miller family legends survive this early Wythenshawe period but one was particularly significant: a tragic accident for Linda. Dancing in her new party dress with friends when her mum had called at May's flat on the same landing, Linda knocked the fireguard away and her dress set alight. For Vee and Hal, it was a complete disaster from which, perhaps, they never fully recovered. Vee always felt the guilt of that two-minute trip to May's door. She said she could never forget the screams. Quick thinking on someone's part saw Linda rolled up in the clippy mat as they waited for the bell-ringing ambulance to arrive. Hospitalisation was inevitable and many operations followed. Linda's skin grafts would constantly mark her approach to life. Fortunately, she was feisty and it was a good job. She made a wonderful recovery and as life continued, it was only wearing a swimming costume that became the long-time loser.

This early tragedy was a real blow, one of many to follow, but it was met with some real resilience. Resilience was a necessary quality in post-war council estates and especially if your name was Vera Miller. School dominated the children's lives. Brian was the clever one. In these early days, Linda was more interested in friends, dressing up and surviving. Vee recalls the day another parent knocked on the flat door. She opened the door to some considerable angry vibes. A large boy showing a swollen black eye was presented. 'Look what your child has done to my Roger!' the furious mother shouted. Vee got set to call Brian out to face the music, only to be told that it was Linda who had done the deed. She had been defending her brother. When Vee presented her dainty daughter with full Shirley Temple ringlets to the mum, the woman decided to leave, somewhat deflated and a little embarrassed. That was Linda. Always ready for the fight and always defending her family, even if she and Brian wouldn't walk on the same side of the road to school.

On a lighter front, Linda always tells the tale of when, with her school friends, she sat at the back of the upper deck on the bus coming home from school. They were messing about, giggling and swearing in teenage style. She was also smoking, arrogantly and provocatively waving the cigarette as she blew out smoke rings. As always, Linda was one of the loudest of the group (or as we would say in Manchester, 'the one with the gob!'). Unfortunately for Linda, that day Hal was the bus conductor, working his way unnoticed by her as he collected the bus fares. He continued up the aisle, rolling and clicking his ticket machine. As he finally reached the girls, Linda came face to face with her dad. A silence fell. Hal took their fares, not acknowledging Linda, but she knew when she got home she would be in for it. And she was. Even though she was his princess, she would not be spared his anger for she had broken two rules. She had been smoking, though Hal took no high moral ground on that score for he smoked like a trooper. More importantly, it was the public nature of her failing – for Hal that was worse. Bad behaviour at home in private was always viewed in the Miller family as a better order than carried out in front of others.

Vee took the kids each week on the bus to see both the mothers in Moss Side. As they got older, it was more like dragging them, but she persisted. It was a long bus ride, especially with two toddlers, and even harder work with reluctant sulking teenagers but she persevered. In fact, she did this for a long time, way beyond Linda and Brian's childhood and teens. Admittedly, they went to Mary Ellen's first and then, with some relief, to Granny Mac's afterwards. It was a ritual into which all the children would be initiated. At least they got a Blue Riband at Mary Ellen's though they preferred the Kit Kat and attention at Granny Mac's.

Hal loved his job on the buses. The Manchester Bus Corporation, Sharston Depot, was a family in itself. His driver and partner in crime, Bill, became a life-long friend and Vee and Bill's wife, Ethel, often teamed up too. Hal was now christened 'Dusty' at work. It was a long-time nickname for Miller, and he soon became known as Dusty all over the estate. To Vee he would remain Hal. He enjoyed his work. He made sure he was turned out immaculately. Old-fashioned collars with studs were *de rigour* and he wore his uniform with pride: shoes polished to a pristine military shine, jacket brushed down, and hair plastered in Brylcreem. A touch of Old Spice finished him off – and sometimes everybody else. But it was better than the Soir de Paris or old ladies' pee-pot of Heywood Street. Above all, the kids loved the bus ticket machine. There were little wheels that set the price and rolls of different tickets. Once the wheel setting was clicked into place, a lever on the side was pulled to push out the ticket. Just to add to the mechanism's fun, there was a punch on the side so tickets could be authorised. The living room was littered with punched tickets. Often Hal had to prise it out of the kids' hands to take it to work. And he had to think up many excuses to get new ticket rolls. There was good camaraderie within the depot's workers which he loved, apart from having his pay docked once for shouting, 'The dead centre of Manchester' as the bus approached the huge Southern Cemetery. I guess not everyone thought it was funny.

With the arrival of child number three, another boy, it felt like they were really on the up for once. Life was finding its own pace and place and they were becoming a proper family. They had a bit of money in their pockets and in Hal's hiding places – bank accounts were not to be trusted. Linda was well recovered. Brian seemed to be doing well at school, with quite an artistic flair, and the baby didn't keep them up all night. Most of all, Mary Ellen was finally knocked off her perch and certainly didn't rule the roost in their home. Hal had finally grown up.

Family relationships are complicated things. Blood can run thick, just as familial love can be easily manipulated. As much as Hal (and Vee, for that matter) was relieved to be out of Mary Ellen's clutches, he couldn't completely cut his ties. She was his mother, after all. And he bore no resentment towards Pa, who in his own inimitable style had always been kind to him. To be fair, until the wedding day bombshell, he would not have expected that Pa was anything but his real dad. In a strange way, he had felt more than liberated with the news that he only half belonged to the clan. His new family status meant he was detached, one step away from the Miller cabal. Now he could reconfigure things on his own terms. Not many of us get this kind of chance, perhaps not many would want it. The vast majority of us merely accept that this is our family, for good or ill. There will be those whose experience of family is so painful that they would wish for another biological home but for many, no matter what they endure, they remain somewhat loyal to their roots. Those who for any reason have cause to doubt their roots often feel there is something missing from them. Even if their adoptive parents have loved and cherished them, they still have a gap that niggles away. It is more than curiosity; it seems to mess with their own self-defining, their own self-expressing, or finding their own identity. Often, they can suppress the feelings for a time, but they will keep bubbling up in dreams or the odd comment. There is a restlessness that will not settle.

Hal (or perhaps Dusty as it now was) had some decisions to make. He had one more try at getting his mother to unlock her sealed lips on the subject, but to no avail; her lips were as tight as the proverbial camel's rear in a sandstorm. However, Vee had a bit of an unexpected breakthrough. Mary Ellen's youngest sister, Elsie had moved to Wythenshawe. She was considerably older than Vee, but much younger than Mary Ellen. Vee hardly knew her, though she did know of her. Vee met her at the market and it was Elsie who made the running. 'Aren't you Vera Macknight? Didn't you marry our Harold?' Soon her tongue was let loose in chatter and her desire to show Vee that she knew more about Mary Ellen than Vee ever could. Knowledge like this is a juicy thing, especially if it makes good gossip. And some people love to dispense it. Elsie certainly did. The bigger the drama, the better.

'You are lucky to have escaped from our Nel,' she said. 'She's always been a bad 'un, she has. Ruled the roost in our house until she caused the scandal of the century on Arnold Terrace. No wonder she did a flit.'

Vee was all ears now. Cue the inevitable question. 'What scandal was that?'

Then it came spilling out. How the young Mary Ellen took off with an older man. She was probably pregnant, at least that is what everybody presumed. The man was from the Jewish community in Cheetham Hill or Prestwich, or around there somewhere. He came to collect her, the Jewish man, but her dad threw her out before he even knocked on the door, clothes and all into the street. She was screaming her head off. That was the last the family saw of her for years. Until she turned up in Heywood Street as Mrs Miller, in fact. What happened in between remained a mystery, or at least a secret Mary Ellen wouldn't tell. Her sister had been just a young girl when it happened and, to be fair, she liked the story and liked telling it.

Vee related all this to Hal. It fed his desire to find out more but he was at a loss as to how he would do that. Anyway, he knew that he had some more urgent work to do.

The kids had all been registered as Millers and their father as Harold Miller. He had to put it right. In truth, he would have been tempted to revert to Maurice Daniels, but the kid's registration had put paid to that. He booked a solicitor's appointment to change his name to Miller by deed poll. And that's what he did. The mystery of Daniels was buried, for a little while longer at least.

CHAPTER 4

With arrival of the new baby, the flat was bursting at the seams. They could cope alright but as Linda and Brian, got older it became impractical for them to be in the same bedroom. This time the Council needed no councillor to persuade them. Vee went to look at the new houses in Peel Hall. They were lush, or some more contemporary word like that. There was still a working farm at the centre, with a big farmhouse, and cows and pigs. It smelt of countryside. Vee could swear she saw pear trees and apple trees and an old water pump. There was also a little school and people talked about a row of shops being built and, of course, a pub. What more could you want? She dreamt they would offer her a house and when they did, she danced for joy, literally.

The house, 165 Ashurst Road, had three bedrooms. To be honest, one was quite small but big enough for one of the kids. They called it the bunk room because it had a large ledge or bunk over the stairs which provided a useful bit of storage space. There was a huge through room downstairs (that's why they called them 'sunshine' houses), a kitchen with a sink and drainer and a brand-new portable boiler for washing, with a dolly stick and some Dolly Blue. The outhouse was really part of the house as it was off the kitchen in the space under the stairs. Near the side door at the end of the outhouse was the coal bunker. It opened on the outside for the coal man to deliver and on the inside to get coal for the house. No more getting wet on cold nights to build up the fire! Luxury, pure luxury. The gardens needed sorting out, but they were there and they backed on to the school playing field. It would be great for Geoff when he was older.

The day they moved in, so did the next-door neighbour and a few others. There was a feeling of optimism, hope and fresh starts in the air. In 163 there was Flo, Reg and two girls: Anne, who was younger than Brian and Linda, and Janice just a few months younger than Geoff. Perhaps they would become friends? The street soon filled up. Alice and Harold Etchells moved in next door to 167 on the other side. They had four kids, and another on the way, and they had old Harold (Alice's father-in-law) with them as well. Next to them were two flats to end the terrace. On the bottom, a Polish family; he was a veteran and had fought with the Allies in the war; and above was Betty Wilmott, her son and a big dog. The dog was called Alchy after her long-gone husband, at least that's what Hal said. Opposite was Maggie Kemp and her six lads. They all worked at the bakery, and with all the different shifts, the comings and goings, the front door was never closed. Maggie soon became the best neighbourhood watch any one could have organised. When not cooking, she sat in her paisley pinny on the flowerbox beside the front door. Before long, Vee got to know them all well, plus the Walkers in the bottom flat next to Maggie's; Sally Walker snooped behind her net curtains, so Hal called her *The News of the World* but she was harmless. The Delaneys, a huge Irish family, lived in the Square next to Mr and Mrs Privett, a local preacher in the Methodist church. The Waterfields were just a few doors away. Margaret liked to come and chat but once she came she didn't always leave easily. Hal called her 'Titty Bud'. He could make up disparaging names for many. They were usually accompanied by naughty ditties which he would sing to the kids' delight and Vee's disgust. 'She's not here again,' he would sigh as he came in. He said it directly to her face (fortunately she laughed) but she was good company for Vera. The Averys lived next door to Flo and Reg. Jean worked in the British Legion Club and was a good contact for getting the kids tickets to the club's Christmas party, which was renowned for being the best. Treats galore and a night of *Looney Tunes*! Flo did some shifts there, too. Jack Avery sang like Matt Monroe, though this was before the time of Karaoke so he never got the backing track he deserved. He also liked a fight, especially after a drink or at a football match. He had a fierce temper which only Jean could control. Best of all was watching him lose it in the Kippax Stand at City's ground on a Saturday afternoon. He certainly widened the kids' vocabulary. And, of course, there was old Ma Buckley who always seemed to be moaning about kids playing on the green (a small square of houses with a green space in the middle: "No Ball Games to be Played here", said the lamppost notice). She perhaps forgot that most of the kids who were playing there were those she was looking after. It seemed quite a street, with lots of children and mixed-aged families but mainly they were young ones like the Millers, just starting out. Halcyon days lay ahead.

Except life has a habit of throwing things at you, left field. But first, a bit of early life on Ashurst Road is worth remembering. Flo became Vera's closest confidante. They shared mugs of tea, news tips and things women share in whispers. This became a common tradition and later proved to be really useful camaraderie. At this stage, it was much about kids talk and domestic matters. Later it would be about the dreaded 'change' and 'the headache' – cue whispers or lips mouthing strange words while listening to the peaceful Mantovani. Flo and Vee would natter but never to excess. The prop banging on the back door to signal rain and therefore time to bring the washing in was also the signal to put the kettle on. The kids got on well, with Geoff and Jan growing up together like twins. In fact, that's what everyone called them: the Bisto twins, like in the advert. They would sit giggling on the step, each with a mop of white-blonde hair. Jan, in a neat little frock and her white ankle socks, was always a little weightier than Geoff, the whippet, in his favourite denim dungarees. Some said it was Geoff's only advantage that, at an early age, he could move faster than her. But Geoff soon learned her other weaknesses, not least how to make her giggle and have to rush indoors to the loo. Of course, she knew his weaknesses too, not least where to tickle and, if nothing else, at this stage she could just sit on him. They say it takes a long time to grow old friends and their friendship started early enough to reach the old friend mark in no time.

It was with Jan that Geoff had his first bath with a woman! (Note, I said "first" – sadly any other such baths remain a guarded secret.) They were not quite three, and it was hardly a bath, more of a wash down in the kitchen sink and a towel dry on the draining board. Even today, it is one of their earliest memories. The reason for the joint washing was that next-door Vee was giving birth to her fourth and last child, Gary. He proved to be a tiny, puny bag of bones just short of 4lbs with a mop of dark curly hair. Too tiny, in fact, for the old crib that had been prepared for him, so he was swaddled and placed in a drawer from the bedroom chest. 'Looks just like his dad,' people would say as they stared at his wrinkled prune-like face staring up from the pram. 'Poor little bugger!' they would add as they put a silver sixpence into his tiny grasping fingers. But things changed: his hair grew and curled, and he put on weight and joined in with all the children who proliferated on the street. Street urchins all of us. They (or *we*, in fact – notice I can now add myself into the story) lived most of the time outside on the street, *our* street. Prams were left outside the front door for afternoon sleeps while mothers smoked, drank tea and told stories. Later, when they were older, kids played on the road, in the woods or on the farm, dodging Farmer Shenton as they climbed his pear trees and removed his unripe, solid pears which would give them a belly ache before tea time. They moved around in droves, sometimes colliding with other groups from nearby streets like Bleak Hey or Wilks Avenue. Sometimes peacefully, but not always. They were not tough gangs like those we often talk of today. No county line drug dealing or mobster activity. Pen knives were really only used to play a game called chicken. You had to stand with legs apart and the knife was thrown to a new spot. If it stuck in the ground, then you had to move your leg to the knife spot. Then you could throw the knife back near your opponent's feet. The first to fall lost. A huge camaraderie and solidarity existed. Even if you were one of the more timid ones, the big 'uns would stand up for you against another group, and if all else failed, there was Aunty Alice.

Alice Etchells was a tiny, puny little firebrand. 'More meat on a butcher's apron' they used to say, but you would be wise to avoid her wrath. Wound up, she uncoiled like a lioness, and especially if it was in defence of her children. She seemed always to be wearing rollers in her hair, covered in a pink scarf, and a smock apron over her dress. Her stockings would be rolled down to the top of her mule slippers that were finished with a bright pink fluffy pom-pom. Perhaps the latter was to match the scarf, but I doubt it. She had a nervous face tic (would you wonder why?), constantly pushing her tongue out of her mouth. Hal reckoned that after a few minutes chatting with her, you found yourself doing the same. She had by now five children: two lads, twin girls and Jeanie, the eldest. (Mind you, she hadn't finished yet). Vee always said that an hour after having the twins, she was putting washing on the line. Her tiny house was full to overflowing with all the kids and the old grandad. Jeanie, the eldest girl, slept in the outhouse and some of the lads slept in the poorly boarded-out attic. The house always smelt of old toast and HP brown sauce. It was, however, a favourite house to play in on a rainy day, especially if you were allowed upstairs. Going upstairs in any other house was a rare thing. Better to have you playing where you could be seen might have been one reason. Yet I think it was the shame of the poor décor and furniture that was probably the real reason. The walls in our house weren't painted for many years, well at least until I took my first friends home from Teacher Training College. My, were they honoured, though I doubt they realised just how much! For most of us, old sprung bedsteads, the odd rickety table and wardrobe or an old chair sufficed. Bedding was a luxury item and, even then, it was often old hospital-style blankets, lumpy eiderdowns and Camberwick striped fleecy sheets. At least they were warm in the winter as there was no heating except in the living room. Every morning we used to wait for the fire to be lit before we ventured downstairs. Dad would use a sheet of newspaper as a 'blower' to speed up the process, but later we got a sheet of thin metal to put across. Floor boards were at best littered with clippy mats and, in some of the houses, newspaper – fresh newspaper, mind. Upstairs in the Etchells' house and especially in the attic, there was barely room to move amid the beds and mattresses. They did, however, make the very best fighting rings for tag matches, springy, bumpy trampolines or primitive bouncy castles.

Aunty Alice was a fierce defender of her kids. We loved it when she was on the war path; her altercations always extended our vocabulary and honed our attack skills.

'Mrs Crabtree's got Babs!' we shouted once. Babs (real name Jimmy) was not the actual baby of the family but the favourite. In a flash, Alice had grabbed her broom and marched around the corner to the Crabtree's house, all the time dispelling threats and expletives that would get us a slap when we repeated them later to Vee. Behind her, a cortege of mocking kids egged her on. It was a pathetic fight in reality for Ma Crabtree backed down almost straightaway – shouting but not putting up much resistance. Babs was quickly liberated to cheers, but Alice needed a pound of flesh. As Ma Crabtree cowered near the open coal house door, Alice pushed her in and bolted it. 'That'll let her cool down for a bit,' she said or words to that effect. Then the diminutive leader, with broom held high, marched back to Ashurst Road with her full retinue behind her, curlers bobbing and her pom-pom mules lighting the way.

*

It wasn't always the desire to go the kids' defence that made her angry. There was a legendary day when, so fed up with all the banging on the piano in the outhouse (the only piano in the street and one that no one but Grandad could even remotely play), she pushed it out into the road and hacked it to pieces. This tiny fireball perched on top, with strings and wood flying off in every direction. Yet this tough old bird reared seven kids, stood by one when he was sent to an approved school for being the daft one who got caught, cared for her elderly father-in-law, and kept the family together when Harold, her husband, died young. This tiny, feisty firebrand, who could let her anger descend on anyone who narked her, was often the first at the door to bring food or help out when things were tough. It was Alice who called every day to ask how Vee was when later she struggled with cancer. She had a hard, difficult life, but she had a heart that was bigger than the frame that held it.

The broken piano made great 'bongy wood' for the Guy

Fawkes bonfire. We collected stuff to burn from everywhere. We loved old settees because of what we might find down the back or sides. We once found an old ma's lost wedding ring! The huge bonfire would be built on the green near the farm. It had to be guarded to stop rival streets setting it alight too early. The Moores lads who lived at the end house near the green were the real security force. On the fifth of November, we would top the bonfire with a home-made Guy Fawkes, eat home-made toffee apples, parkin cake and treacle toffee. The latter was not good for the teeth or any fillings. The men lit fireworks and the older scally wags tried to frighten people with bangers. It wasn't Vee's favourite night and her Linda experience meant she kept a close watch on the kids. We loved it, the dogs less so.

The kids on the street shared everything (not least chicken pox and German measles). Sally Walker made packets of sugar with oats, others chopped pomegranates in half and gave them out with a pin to pick; rhubarb and sugar dip was another favourite and there was always custard pie from Maggie. Summers seemed long and warm, punctured with huge games of rounders on the field, with parents taking their turns to bat and run. Margaret Waterfield was a star, easily running from base to base, though she made sure everyone had a go, little and large, young or old, weak or strong. There was no rounders bat, just a battered tennis racket and a few old tennis balls. Men played darts outside Maggie's front door. It was a favourite of Hal's. The six bakery lads were always up for competition, usually with a small wager involved. A wager Hal invariably won. There were other crazes that seemed to come from nowhere and disappear just as fast. Marbles (we called them allies), stilt walking and 'can walking' (two cans with string threaded through them; you would stand on the can and hold the string and attempt to walk), depending on which you get your hands on. Roller skates if you were rich or there was a pair to be found in the outhouse, conkers (without protective glasses), 'two ball' against the wall, and skipping. We played 'Kick Can', 'What time is it Mr Wolf?' and my favourite, 'The big ship sailed through the alley, alley O'. Best of all was making and racing 'bogey carts'. They were made out of old pram wheels, a plank and an orange crate, either nicked from Mr Jones the greengrocer or brought home from the bakery. We had no real tools in our house and so Hal had to bore a hole in the plank using a red-hot poker. We all gathered around to watch this amazing feat. The steering stick was threaded through and attached to the front wheels and some attached rope provided the steering device. We painted and decorated them, giving them crazy names such as 'Crasher', 'Striker', 'Devil-dash'.

It was best when we could ride our carts at the foster home, the house at the end of the terrace. Being at the end, it had more drive space and a steeper slope. You could easily go faster, starting at the top and turning right past the privet into the street. There was a notorious occasion when Gary – in 'Dasher' – came hurtling down the slope with a crowd watching. One person was timing the descent. Geoff had commandeered a bit of an old mop which he held to his mouth like a microphone while he was screaming a running commentary. As 'Dasher' turned the corner, it crashed into 'Mrs Quarange'. This was really Ma Goode, (known as Mrs Quarange following an animated character used for advertising Robinson's juice) and fortunately she was not hurt that much. She could handle herself anyway (she had four lads of her own). She berated us and said she would be having words with our mam. It was all made worse by the crowd who were quietly humming the advert jingle as we looked suitably repentant. Vee had other ideas and marched us across to the green where Ma Goode lived and made us give humble apologies. 'If they get up to any further monkey business, May, then tell me and I'll do more than knock their bloody heads together,' she declared. Though afterwards, she laughed with us (a little bit) and told us that it was always best to apologise when we were in the wrong. She advised us that a proper apology 'wrong foots' the anger.

Hal was a favourite with the kids. His spellbinding tricks could produce little packets of XL chewing gum from behind your ears. We queued up to watch and get our packets of gum. Aunty Flo was a demon with the sewing machine and made Jan a nurse's outfit and Geoff a white doctor's coat. She and Vee were a bit shocked when they watched the two of them performing a 'Caesarean birth' of a doll from the blanket-covered belly of Corinne Avery. Of course, they didn't use the word 'Caesarean' but they had worked out for themselves that a baby in a tummy had to come out somehow. Their imagination would constantly get the better of their parents.

Vee was wonderful at roleplaying. She could turn the living room into a library with a counter and a date stamp to boot, or into an interior of a charabanc with proper tickets and even a driving wheel at the front. Picnics on the fields were a treat and didn't need to consist of much more than jam butties. All the kids from the street came along. There were long walks along Styal Road to the airport to watch the planes coming and going, or to Styal Woods past the thatched cottage whose chimney Hal swept each year, and on to look at all the posh houses. (Vee always liked the bungalow called 'Mylittleheaven', with no spaces between the words.) Sometimes they would stop and buy fresh green apples from a farm along the way, occasionally a lemonade for the kids and a shandy for the adults at the Ship Inn in Styal. It all happened, and lots more, and for the best part, people got on. Vee had a rule never to fall out about the kids. 'By the time you've argued, they are friends again,' she would say. Though of course, it wasn't always the case.

It would be more than misleading to suggest that this was a sun-coated, working class, socialist utopia. There was a darker side that too often reared its head and seemed always to simmer underneath, breaking out without warning or favour. Many was the night punctured with drunken raucous men – usually, in fact, almost always men – singing, shouting and fighting in the street in the early hours. Too often upstairs, bedroom windows would open and vomit would ejaculate onto the street from a husband worse for wear. Too often women scurried to the shops with their bruised faces hidden from sight, but their loyalty to drunken brutes was never called into question. After all, they had the kids to think of and no income of their own except some occasional pin money.

Certainly not enough to live on. There were even darker secrets not to be talked about except at home, behind closed doors and even then in whispers. Incest and sexual abuse were not publicly tolerated but were certainly known about. Some fathers were grandfathers to the same children – just ask the MacFaddens on Holly Road, or don't if you are not prepared to be repulsed and horrified in much the same measure.

The Youngs, who lived in the square, were a different example of the darker shadow of some families' lives. The day the bailiffs called still makes those who remember it shudder. Large men in black busted into the house while Ma Young, her kids gathered all around her and pulling on her apron, cried on the doorstep. The house was emptied onto the green for all to see. Not much was worth taking away. Piles of rickety, dilapidated furniture and bags of clothes, pots and pans were thrown onto the green, heaping more humiliation on the sobbing mam and her kids. Mrs Young scurried off with the kids to her sister's house, which was around the corner. Vee said there would surely be trouble when Mr Young came home. He had been giving his wife the rent money each week, but the Bingo proved too tempting and the money slipped through her fingers. Poverty is a cruel master and was never far from the surface in most households.

Vee knew enough about life not to judge others in their plight. Like when a girl called Sharon at school got pregnant. She was barely fifteen. Vee said, 'Easy done, everyone makes mistakes. Just you wait and see.' It was the same with Ma Young and the bailiffs. Vee knew we were just a step away from a similar fate. That thought came home to roost when Hal stood guarantor for his brother John. John had defaulted on the payments, and it brought those same black-suited bully boys to our door. We weren't turfed out of the house 'cos Vee always paid the rent. Instead, the cowboys just ransacked the house. In reality there wasn't much worth taking but what there was they did. Flo, Alice, Jean and Margaret joined forces to console a crying Vee at the front door. Then they set to work to salvage what was left. 'It's not too bad,' they chorused. 'You'll manage, you always do.' We, the kids, just hated seeing Vee cry. Hal couldn't bear it.

I always think of Vee's non-judgemental personality, learnt through a tough and flawed life experience, when I read the biblical story in John Chapter 8. The story of the woman caught in adultery. Vee wouldn't have known the story then, though she would have shared my anger at the fact that it was the woman and not the man who bore the brunt of the crowd's anger. What I think of, though, is that little phrase somewhere in the middle of the story when Jesus challenges the mob. 'Let he who is without sin throw the first stone,' he declares, and the text goes on to say that, one by one, they leave. And here's the rub: the text continues, 'and the oldest left first'. Honest reflection on one's own life invariably leads to more compassion. As Hal would say, 'When you point one finger forward, two face backwards towards you.'

In truth, Hal and Vee weren't the best at home budgeting. To be fair, they didn't have much with which to budget. Hal liked counting his money in secret and stashing it away; Vee would worry about money, but it slipped through her fingers. She rarely spent it on herself. They had some very low moments too, worse than most.

Hal had long looked forward to passing his driving test to move into the bus driving seat. It would involve a much welcomed pay increase. However, fortune had a different path for him to follow. Vee was cooking for the kids – chips, their favourite. With remarkable speed, she chipped some potatoes directly into a large pan of bubbling fat. Soon they would be golden crisp on the outside and soft and fluffy on the inside. Accompanied by a fried egg, they always made Wednesday's tea special. Hal was due in from his late shift any time, and she had one lamb chop ready to cook for him in the scullery cupboard. It was his favourite. He was late, then later, then very late, then worryingly late. A knock on the door brought his workmate and shift gaffer. Harold was in hospital; he had 'fallen' at work. In a panic, Vee put on her coat and headscarf. She got Flo to look after the kids and set off with Bill the gaffer to the local hospital. The accident, however, was not really an accident at all. It seemed Hal had suffered a fit of some kind. He had fallen and thrashed around on the floor, grunting and taking deep breaths. People had gathered round, trying to help him, but as he came around he remembered nothing. It was a savage blow. In the hospital bed, he looked broken. He wore a blue hospital gown and a huge, very swollen black-eye, one of many black-eyes that followed the fits that Vee would witness in the years to come. He could never just fall where he was – it was always down the stairs, into the fireplace or onto the toilet pan. For now, trying to process this new and painful experience, he was distraught, a little confused and bewildered, unsure what was happening to him. He was not an easy patient, well, not until they prescribed enough drugs to settle him down. It would take more than heavy sedation to get him (or Vee) through the years ahead. Tests seemed somewhat inconclusive and further fits followed in quick succession: a brainstorm caused by pain, a form of epilepsy, all were mentioned, all were frightening and all were devastating. Hal would never pass that driving test, but he would lose more than that particular dream all in a moment of a blasted, unwanted brainstorm. In time (not that long, in fact) he would be 'let go' by the Bus Corporation (there's not much use for a bus conductor with the threat of a fit hanging over him and the safety of fare-paying passengers). With the loss of the job would come further loss: a loss of self-confidence, a loss of identity and, of course, a loss of regular income. Too quickly the family would also learn that there was more to fits like this than the fear of a debilitating illness or wrecked future dreams. Some people were frightened in his presence. The almost biblical, primitive ideas of curses and devils took a modern form with people scared when they witnessed this thrashing, manic Hal, frothing and grunting on the floor before them. For Hal, the world was falling apart. It was a new landscape that he found hard to configure, never mind navigate.

Vee had other concerns, more immediate ones. Hal in hospital with his job on the line meant she was wondering how to manage without any cash. It would take some time to sort sick pay and benefits out, but she had to manage until then. There were friends who would help, but she had had enough humiliation telling others for now, even going cap in hand to Flo. In the kitchen she had a half a loaf, a few eggs and a bag of potatoes which would last them less than a week. She walked the few miles to the hospital to visit Hal and used what little cash she could find to buy him a bottle of Lucozade and his Capstans, both bright orange she mused as she put them on his locker. She kept the Lucozade wrapping for the kids. Wrapped around a comb, it made a brilliant Kazoo. It would keep them quiet for a while at least, though the noise would be a nuisance.

In a short time, Hal was looking better, calmer and not quite so drugged up. He was lucid, too, for once.

'How you managing, Vee? Have you got enough cash?'

'Don't worry, I'll manage.'

'Well, if you get stuck there's a fiver in my old suit in the wardrobe. It's in the ring pocket, folded tight.'

Cue sausages for tea, lots of them, and a large tin of marrowfat peas. Tins of peas were a good bet because you could place the open tin in the oven to warm up. Saved on the washing up, in truth, but essential when you had hardly any cooking pans to begin with. Hal was still secreting his private stash for a rainy day, a habit he would continue until his dying day.

The Millers' world reconfigured, hardly noticed by the little ones, but demanding every bit of energy that Vee could muster.

CHAPTER 5

Certainly, Hal was diminished, changed. If nothing else, he stopped wearing his false teeth, which might be good for a gurning competition but not for street life. But looking back, I think it was a statement. (He'd had all his teeth out as a twenty-first birthday present to himself. He'd paid sixpence for the quack dentist to come and pull each one as he lay on the kitchen table.) Soon people got used to him without teeth; his hollowed-out cheeks seemed to grow to fill in the space. His gums were hard – he could eat an apple without cutting it up. Geoff and Gary can't really remember him with his teeth in, bar two occasions, well, almost three: Linda's wedding (then they only lasted until the wedding tea), the consecration of the new church (but people did not recognise him or understand him as he spoke like a radio not quite tuned in), and then the "almost" when the funeral directors were keen to put them in as he lay in his coffin (we stopped them as by then it was too late to worry what he looked like and we loved him as he was).

Vee got a few shifts at the school nearby. Albert the caretaker and his wife Elsie, who lived in the school house just at the end of the terrace, were really helpful. Vee also managed a part-time job as a barmaid at the new Peel Hall pub near the shops. But Hal was uneasy that her Marilyn Monroe peroxide hair and glossy red lips (just like Kathy

Kirby: lipstick and a bit of Vaseline) were too tempting, even in what was then an upmarket establishment. Besides, Vee didn't really like the late nights. Edith Osborne from Glenby Avenue (her with the massive brood of big lads who lived near the Carsons, whose girl lost her leg in a terrible accident) got her a job cleaning in one of the posh houses off Styal Road. She stayed there for years with Mrs Meredith, who was a kindly enough old lady but ultimately quite mean. She paid Vee cash-in-hand and because of that she never put the wages up. She was condescending in offering bits of leftover joints rather than waste them, but not a pay rise. She 'took a lend', Vee said. However, it paid the rent and didn't affect Hal's pittance of a benefit on the sick. Vee soon played her at her own game.

'Shall we stop for a morning drink?' Mrs Meredith asked.

Vee had watched Lorraine Chase in an advert.

'How lovely! I'll have a Campari and lemonade,' she retorted.

In truth, she wasn't much fussed but she got a taste for it as well as the occasional G&T.

Finances were always tight, but slowly the Millers picked themselves up and tried to start again. Hal did the odd casual shift at the bakery, but in truth it was too much for him and they all paid the consequences of set-backs, hospitalisation and sorting out the benefits again. Soon he was more than addicted to Diazepam tablets and couldn't manage a day without them. They caused him to sleep deeply each afternoon and be awake all night. One simple break came when Leo, one of Maggie's lads, was offered promotion to shift manager. He didn't tell the management that he couldn't read or write and that he struggled with maths. Once a month, Leo smuggled Hal on the nightshift so that Hal could do the monthly returns and Leo did the graft. He was glad of the pay. His only other flurry into money making at this stage was to act as a bookie's runner, behind the shops near the garages. The bookie was acting illegally by taking bets from a runner. Hal loved his horse bets, so he used to secretly take the bets of local men and hand them over to the bookie. The bookie's runners could be found in a whole variety of places: factory floors, local pubs and the like. They were common on big housing estates that were too far from the bookmaker's premises. The runner was paid a small percentage of the bets that he took. As was almost inevitable, Hal got busted and took the punishment. The fine was fortunately paid by the bookie, but Vee wasn't happy that Hal continued as a runner.

Of course, they were not alone in struggling with their money. For most families, there were few ways to beat off the debt, but debt smoked its way like a pernicious fume, seeping into almost every family home. Catalogue purchases meant accounts proliferated. People chose the latest dress or shoes but couldn't keep up with the payments, resulting in bitter fall-outs among would-be friends.

There were three other means of luring you into spending money you didn't always have on a weekly basis:

Firstly, the Providential, or the "Provi" as it was known, gave you a cheque to spend in certain shops and then extorted weekly amounts to cover the cost. Plus, an exorbitant interest. You could easily catch the Provi man on his rounds, knocking at locked doors as people hid inside to avoid a payment.

Then there were the clubmen. Ours was Mr Potts, a large, amiable old chap who wore a dark Macintosh, shiny black shoes and a titfer hat which he raised at the door and took off if he came inside where he kept it on his knee. He visited in his van, which was like an Aladdin's cave. If he didn't have what you wanted, you could ask him and he would do his best to access it for the next visit. Sadly, he didn't always get it right, but often 'almost right' had to be good enough. This all led to pleasure but sometimes huge disappointment. Most of all, there was little choice. Payback was weekly and interest was not as bad as the Provi but it was still interest, and taken with a polite smile. In later years, he modernised by giving you a little chitty which you would take to a warehouse in Cheetham Hill and choose the item for yourself – from their limited range, of course. It was so limited in range that when it came to clothes, you could see what next year's choice would look like just by casting an eye along the clothes rack. At least there was a choice and you could try it on to possibly get a reasonable fit.

Maggie had two or three different clubmen. She had huge accounts with them, often in different names, some fictional and some not, paying each week just enough to make sure the clubman couldn't give up on her. Often what she got from the clubman was immediately hawked along the street to raise cash: cheap sheets, bales of towels, small electrical objects and the like. Sometimes, brazenly, she would take an order and come back to you with it when the clubman visited the next week. I think she worked on the basis that she only paid one of them each week. Often, she would shout over, 'Vee, if you happen to see Mr Simpson, the clubman, could you tell him I was called out and he'll have to call back next week?' The excuses wore thin, but she owed so much that he had little option but to persevere or give up the ghost and lose the lot.

Finally, and perhaps the most troubling, there was Mr Smythe, a shy man, well dressed, gently and politely spoken. He always came at night. He was not alone but his 'partner' remained at the gate in the shadows. Smythe was the money lender. Out of his suit pocket, he would produce a wad of notes and his little book. You could borrow £15, and then you paid back a pound a week for twenty weeks. You had to pay the first week straight away, so he only handed over nineteen pounds. Failure to pay a week added two weeks, so for £15, you could be in debt for weeks and weeks to come. People rarely missed payments. To be honest, I never heard of any violence, but there was an understanding that you didn't mess about with him – not even Maggie dared. By some bizarre logic, Hal paid him a pound each week even if he didn't have a 'loan on the go'. 'Best to keep the facility available,' Hal said. 'You never know when you might need some cash.'

A possibility sometimes was to take in a lodger. When Petrochemicals were building at Trafford Park, there was an army of contract workers looking for digs. Vee cleared the boxroom and tidied it up as best she could. The first upstairs room to be painted! It was cheap magnolia from the market but it was clean. 'Mr Clegg to you' lodged with us for a while. He had a car which, apart from Uncle Jack Waterfield's

Meccano-set of a wreck in the garden, became only the third car on the street. We thought we had won the pools when we went on a trip with the whole family to see the Blackpool lights, all squashed in his black Hillman Humber. Otherwise, we rarely saw him. We were banned from the kitchen when Vee served his supper, and occasionally she would cut off a bit of the steak to go with Hal's sausage. He helped pay the bills, but sadly it wasn't long before his contract was over and he returned, like he did each weekend, to his family in Yorkshire. At least Brian got his room back and there was more space for Gary and Geoff in the double bed.

Some of these lodgers on the street, however, chose to stay. Jud, an overweight cockney, became firmly ensconced at Maggie's. He was of the labouring, poorer paid type, and wasn't so keen on hiking back to the old smoke. He got on well in the Higginbottom house, so much so that – to everyone's surprise and delight – he announced that he was to be married to Maggie. She was dolled up to the nine pins with an old brown fur coat and a hat she had borrowed with a little black veil. She gave a new twist to one of Hal's disparaging comments, usually said about people from the private estate: 'All fur coat and no knickers.' With that, a new dress from the clubman and a bit of lippy the deed was done. The kids were fascinated with the black taxi that took them to the Register Office. Most of all, they loved the pennies thrown out to all and sundry as the happy couple clambered aboard. Of course, there was a party that night in the club, and then into the early hours on the street. Jud soon became part of the street's legends. Every day he collected the men's bets and took them to the local bookies at the slowly developing Civic Centre. I suppose he was a different kind of bookie's runner, more legit and not paid by the bookie, though he usually got a tip from any winnings which kept him in baccy.

Other possibilities for combatting debt were small beer, really, but they helped at least a little bit. A tab at the Co-op (account number 35691) meant you got dividend as well. There were loads of street vans hawking their wares and providing a structure to the week. Each had their own set days. Driving his little electric van, the milkman sold eggs, wonderful full-orange juice (in milk bottles, too) and bread, along with his daily delivery of milk. Of course, Maggie sold bread straight from the bakery, which was cheaper. Soapy Sam, the hardware man selling Brillo pads, washing up liquid and Dolly Blue to make your whites shimmer, came on Wednesdays. He was a very ardent Jehovah's Witness, frightening some women with end-of-the-world conspiracies, though to most he was a simple soul who liked to talk. On Saturdays, the Rib Man called. He was a favourite. He sold full sheets of ribs and wonderful ham shanks, pigs trotters and tripe. For the likes of us, he saved bags of 'scraps and bits' which made soup, and the meatier ones were boiled and served with mash at Saturday lunch time. Hunt the meat was a favourite game as the pools results came in. Every other day, John the baker would call round. He became a family friend, providing Hal with some welcome male conversation in the long days without work. He'd stay for a cup tea and a chat. He had the most delicious bilberry tarts topped with a circle of cream with a hole in the middle, just big enough for a tongue to taste the bilberry underneath or a finger if you didn't mind not relishing the moment slowly and finishing quicker.

For Hal, the days and weeks began to settle into a fresh routine. It helped him cope with the humiliation of no longer providing for his family. Mornings were spent studying form and picking his favourites for the daily bet. It was the same money that he used each day to make his daily kitty. *One pound and five pence tax paid* was what you wrote at the bottom of the tab. For that, he would choose either a Yankee, an Accumulator or just a plain Each-Way. At the end, he placed his lucky *nom de plume* 'HMV 165'. Jud would collect it about 12.30, in good time for the first afternoon race. By tea time, he would know the results and the next day collect his winnings or drown his sorrows. He never won, or at least that's what we were supposed to believe. However, we knew the signs. Jud would arrive and they would disappear into the kitchen with hushed talking. The longer they were, there the more he had won. When he won big, we would all get a treat, a new ball or a hairdo for Vee. Rare but happy occasions.

The afternoon brought him prescription drugs (mainly Valium and Diazepam) which put him to sleep but kept the curse of fits at bay for a time. Any spare time he had, he would sit on the flower box and watch the world go by, mug of tea in hand. Everybody knew him and everybody stopped to chat. He was in his own way a local legend, doling out hard-earned wisdom littered with raucous and risqué (though not too risqué) humour. In the evenings, he would sit in his chair at the side of the fire, Vee in the opposite chair. She would knit while we, the kids, sat on the floor at her side.

Click, click, click went the needles. She stopped only to look through our hair for a different kind of nits. The telly boomed away, rarely being turned off. It was a huge telly, not in screen size but in the tube at the back. On hire from Rediffusion, it had a meter attached which ate coins and they usually ran out of time just at the critical moment in the programme we were watching. There were just the two channels which you tuned into with a dial. Sometimes it took forever, with whistling and quivering fuzzy lines depending on the arial, which was often made with a coat-hanger and needed moving around until we got a reasonable picture. For a while, we couldn't afford the TV licence and so one of us would sit at the window watching for the detector van. I don't think we ever got caught. We loved *Bootsy and Snudge*, *Morecombe and Wise* and *The Rag Trade*. Hal preferred *Z Cars* and Vee *Emergency Ward 10*. A whole family favourite would be *Miss World* which we watched usually with a little wager on the side. Sometime later, it was *Juke Box Jury*, then *Top of the Pops* with the 'Go-Go' girls, and *Saturday Night at the London Palladium*. On big nights like *Miss World* or *The Royal Variety Show*, there would be treats from the 'offie' (a little counter shop at the side of the pub) which sold cigarettes and chocolate bars. When we went to bed, Hal often woke up. He slept for a while on the living room rug, allowing Vee to jump in to bed with Gary and Geoff or Linda. By early morning, he would have crossed the road to Maggie's. Some of the lads would be on the way home from their shift and Maggie cooked breakfast for anyone and everyone. Here he was at home as part of the family; here he became arbiter in the craic, which often descended into petty but loud arguments. Hal was trusted as 'the one who knew' and he could settle things down before they escalated too much. It wasn't what he'd hoped for, but for now it was a life. Vee and the others needed a bit of rest and stability.

CHAPTER 6

Meanwhile, the kids were growing fast. It took Vee and Flo all their wits to keep Jan and Geoff, desperate to join the others, out of the school queue just a few doors away from their houses. There was relief all around when they were finally able to start at school. It was a happy school and they soon settled, relishing every day and loving their teachers: Mrs Edge, Miss Scally, Mrs Lawson and the head, Miss Allen, who took a shine to both of them. They had an expansive and sometimes infuriating imagination, but the teachers appreciated it. Gary followed quickly after. He was less looking forward to school and took a while to settle, but old Miss Parks worked wonders with him and managed to help him re-find his cheeky self.

Linda had already left school. Vee got her a job in an upmarket grocer in Gatley. She hated it: 'Madam this, and madam that' when she was really 'Luv this, luv that', or worse if she was in that kind of mood. She left in no time after losing it with 'a snotty-nosed customer' – her words to Vee. She got a job straight away at the Smith's crisps factory, it meant free crisps, in blue and white packets, with a little blue screwed up paper inside containing the salt. She loved factory work (and crisps) but was tempted away from there to work at a factory closer to home: Thomas French's, who made curtain tape that was branded as Rufflette. Paid piecework rates, she was a grafter, she earned well and she loved it. She loved, and screamed at, Cliff Richard and the Shadows so much that we dreaded them being on *Top of the Pops*, and of course she idolised Elvis. Her favourite 'street peddler' was Toni's ice cream van, not for the ice cream but for Gianni, the supposedly Italian lad who drove it and sold the ice cream, but who always offered more to the pretty girls he encountered. Hal watched like a hawk. She and her friends would spend ages at the front of the queue, distracting him with their flirting and giggling much to everyone's annoyance, especially Mrs Wilmot, who just wanted her bowl filled with three scoops of vanilla, a good spread of strawberry blood juice on top and, occasionally as a treat, a chocolate flake.

Brian was ready to leave school anytime now, all grown up. He was offered a place at art college. He did well in his UCLI exams and walked into a job in a photography printing shop in the centre of Manchester. Inspired by the Beatles and The Dave Clarke Five, he was really into music and his own band: The Manish Boys. Hardly the next boy-band of the day, but it suited his larger-than-life ego to be the front singer. Weekends were spent mainly at a club called the Twisted Wheel. He was handsome, so they said, and Vee often had to help him dodge between dates. He was set to be the best Mod on the street, but he had itchy feet.

Amid all this, you might have been misled to think that Mary Ellen was an absent player and to presume that, with good grace or not, she had bowed out of meddling in the lives of Hal and Vee, but you couldn't be more wrong. Quite what she really wanted other than to feed the drug of control is hard to establish. Family skirmishes seemed to make her feel alive. It was as if Hal had broken some unwritten cosmic rule to upset her world order and challenge the matriarchy. It couldn't be left alone, it needed to be sorted. To boot, Mary Ellen wasn't a quitter, and playing her hand, like being in control, was in her waters and her blood. She didn't know how to give up, and even though control seemed to have slipped from her flabby fingers, she wasn't done yet.

Dutifully, with a heavy heart and a resigned air, Vee still visited with the younger kids. Gary hated going to Mary Ellen's. He didn't like the musty pee smell, the enveloping and claustrophobic embrace and the whiskers tickling his little face during the dreaded wet kiss. He was so traumatised that on a special treat to see Father Christmas at John Lewis he was convinced it was a disguised nana that approached him. Those whiskers filled him with dread and a big red coat did nothing to calm him. It was like a reverse Little Red Riding Hood story: 'Oh what big whiskers you have got!'

'What can Santa Claus get for you, little boy?' asked the innocent and amiable Father Christmas. He was in his special grotto, which was dark and glittery and all the scarier for it. Queues of parents with children waited for Gary to receive his present and move off for their turn.

'Can I have a Red Indian axe?' he shouted in full squawky kid voice. 'And then I will cut your bleedin' head off!' The Mary Ellen effect clearly had an impact on the kids! Vee scurried away, trying not to laugh, to brave it out. The other mothers and grandmothers stared and tutted and moved up the queue. All parents get used to their kids embarrassing them. (They can usually get their own back at some point: cue baby photograph album and new girlfriend.)

Geoff was more retrospective: quiet and polite but itching to get to Granny Mac's and the Kit Kats. Mary Ellen had learnt one lesson: she could not get to Hal through Vee; she had burnt her boats there and offending Vee would only cause more tears. She would have to skip a generation. But her instinct thought that first a little charm offensive might be best. She let it gestate for a while; she was in for the long game and there was a lot that could happen in the planning time.

I often wondered whether Mary Ellen really planned things, whether she had a strategy or a vague ruse up her sleeve or whether it was just intuitive, a way of being that she rarely reflected upon as she acted. Matriarchal (and, more than likely, patriarchal) family members often seem to work in the same way. As if it were old, deeply rooted wiles that were passed from one generation to another. Perhaps the rebels in the family worked in similar ways, too. Tyranny and protest are always bed partners, and sadly, revolution often just turns the tables rather than resetting the norm. Fortunately, Hal was more liberated, but then he had Vee to keep him on track. Occasionally, I think Hal wondered if he did the old bird a disservice. Forced her into a role or, at worse, demonised her. Just maybe she wasn't so bad and just couldn't help herself. It was usually at that point that he let his guard down, and 'kerplat', she struck. What was true was that wherever she intervened, there was trouble and, as Hal would say, 'Trouble with a capital B.'

She was right when she said a lot could happen in a short time. You didn't have to tell Vee that it was the unlucky story of her life. The next so-called happening started in Talbot Street on one of those family pilgrimages that Vee made, courtesy of the Manchester Bus Corporation. Granny Mac was poorly and Vee was not altogether happy with her brother John and his wife Doreen's care. 'She could come to mine to give you two a rest,' she offered diplomatically. Granny Mac was relieved to get out of the town and she gladly went to Wythenshawe for fresh air and a change of scenery. Plus, she loved being with the little ones who adored her too. It was mutual affection, not based on action or reward. She had little to give them and not enough energy to play, just pure sweet devotion. A bed was put in the living room at the far end, a bed which she hardly ever left. She weakened quickly, her breathing laboured, and there were terrible coughing bouts. Geoff and Gary loved sitting on her bed and helping her to peel grapes, for she believed they needed peeling before eating. A laborious task but they would do anything for her. She talked as they worked and sometimes sang a ditty. In reality, she was not yet sixty, but she looked old, very old, and each day she seemed to sink into the bed. The tall slim woman she had been disappeared before their very eyes. Hal was great and she loved him to bits. He often did the caring while Vee was out cleaning in the posh house on Styal Road. At least Vee got a Campari there.

The old commode came in handy. For the first time, it found its proper use rather than the nearest thing to a wardrobe in the back bedroom, and sometimes a nurse called to give an injection. There were visits from Vee's brothers and sisters because soon they realised that she was too poorly to go back home. John and Doreen blamed Vee for Granny Mac's growing affliction and later blamed Linda as a bug carrier, something that hurt Vee deeply, a blame that would lead to a life-long fracture between them. Looking back, Vee said that it was always bad luck to bring a bed into the living room. It signalled something dark and she shuddered when she thought about it. Granny Mac died not long after. In the later stages, she was taken to the chest hospital in Baguley (the sanitorium), which was an old prisoner of war camp just near the general hospital. It's hard to recall all that happened, but I guess the kids were shipped off to Flo's most of the time. What is easy to recall is the puffed-up, sad red eyes of their mum as she tried to reassure them it would be okay. There was a lot of coming and going, cars at the door, strangers, uncles, aunts and cousins. There was huge excitement as Elsie flew in from America, her first visit home for many years. She had a lot of catching up to do.

Elsie had shiny patent leather shoes, a fragrant flower smell and a lilting American accent. Sweets were called 'candy' and the taps 'faucets'. By this time, she had accommodated a long American drawl and they hardly knew what tomatoes and potatoes were when she spoke. Vee, Hal and the others laughed. The kids on the street were convinced she was a film star and a few even thought that they should curtsy when she offed them a Polo Fruit. Though, of course, in her hands they had magically become this wonderful thing called 'candy', 'candy' with a full American drawl that they all tried to copy.

Death and funerals had their own rituals that began by ceremoniously closing all the curtains in the house. This signalled to the world (or the street, at least) that something dreadful had happened. The house looked like it was declaring the arrival of the plague and it might as well have been. Flo and Jean arranged a collection door to door. It would be used to buy flowers while the rest would go towards the funeral tea. I guess before life insurance societies it was to help cover the costs. In Granny Mac's case, there was enough family to meet the costs and avoid what Granny Mac had had to resort to for her husband who had died years earlier: the dreaded, humiliating pauper grave. For the most part, the family sat around the living room in the almost dark, staring at the empty bed. The lads (Bill and John) sorted the arrangements out and a ham salad tea (It was always ham salad at weddings and funerals. Don't ask why! Although quiche was still firmly in Lorraine) was arranged for afterwards at the local pub. Kids didn't attend, in fact, we were all but banished, farmed out to neighbours to let the family get on with the morbid business. On the funeral day, all the houses in the street closed their curtains out of respect. The flowers were placed on the pavement outside the house and then filled the hearse when it arrived with the coffin and the funeral cars. Everyone was in black and the top-hatted director walked the cortege out of the street for the journey to the cemetery. It felt like in no time all the fuss was over. Elsie had flown back to America with her 'faucets' and 'candy' intact. The visitors drifted away and the bed was removed back upstairs where it belonged. The only lingering memory was the black armbands worn by the men and boys for the next few weeks. The women gathered around Vee, as always, dishing out their own recipes of gossip, kindness, advice and lots of cups of tea and sympathy.

One disaster often follows another. Vee could read that in the tea leaves, which she did regularly for the other women. She was quite convincing, too, as she swirled the last dregs and let the leaves settle at the bottom of the cup, and though she might occasionally have felt an ominous threat in the air, she wasn't expecting this one. Linda took bad. It started with a cold that seemed to go onto her chest. Then, just like Granny Mac, the cough developed, hacking and throaty, as painful to listen to as to bear. The green phlegm, the loss of weight, the shortness of breath. The doctors tried various things, but after X-rays thought it best that she followed Granny Mac into the Baguley Sanitorium. The family were tested too, for tuberculosis. Geoff proudly displayed the ring of little injection pinpricks to his mates, much to Vee's disgust. 'Best keep this quiet,' she said, 'as people will think they will catch something off you.' Linda, sadly, was very poorly. At first, face-to-face hospital visiting was not allowed. Instead, Vee often walked over the fields just to wave to Linda through the window. Eventually, the strict regime was relaxed a little, and they were allowed to meet in a small café run by the WRVS on the hospital site. Linda's strength improved slowly and Vee was tortured yet again by her girl's pain. There was a little hope on the horizon, but Vee knew such hope was always frail. On a brighter note, Linda had fallen in love, headline and sinker. Irvine lived not far away and had worked with Maggie's lads. Hence, he went to Maggie's house to play darts and mess around. I think he met Linda at the ice cream van but maybe that's a false memory: she would have been too busy flirting with the dark Gianni of vague and dubious Italian roots. Irvine Ashworth could not have been more different. Ash, as he was known, was tall and slim with a mop of blonde hair that flopped over his forehead so that he had to keep pushing it back. He was a butcher (or trainee butcher), which made him a good asset for meat lovers, but it also made him picky about the cuts of meat that he would eat. For some reason, he would never touch a sausage. He became a regular at the Millers', and, more importantly, he beat Gianni at the courting game. Linda was besotted. So, as a kind of pick-me-up-cum-something-to-work-towards, Hal said he would agree to their marriage when Irvine had his twenty-first birthday (in those days, you had to get your parents' consent if you were under twenty-one and Ash was three years older than Linda.) It certainly helped and bit by bit Linda regained her health and her feistiness. I think Ash was glad on both counts, though I am only definitely sure on one of them.

Two days after Ash's twenty-first birthday, they were to be married in the Methodist Church near the Civic Centre. The church was chosen even though they didn't have any real connection. Linda had been a Sunday School teacher for a while at the Philadelphia Tabernacle on Crossacres Road, but that was just a hut, not even as good as the Anglican mission hall. St Luke's, the proper parish church, was across the road from the Benchill Pub where they would have the reception. Hal was determined he would have at least a bit of a ride in the taxi. 'We've bloody well paid for them, so we should get our money's worth,' he pontificated.

Before the big day, there were quite a few things to do and Vee thought they should start with some decorating. Vee was the decorator: she could paper and paint, though in the house it had been so far limited to the living room. 'That will need freshening up as well,' she said, looking at the nicotine-stained wallpaper. She went for an orange pattern on the fire-breast and an off-white emulsion to top the new anaglypta on the other walls. Orange was all the rage at the time and the big swirly patterns with browns and the odd bit of green looked clean and crisp. She couldn't afford new curtains, but she would get new nets from the market. First, the old paper had to be stripped and the woodwork washed down. Wall stripping was usually a street affair, especially for the army of kids who piled in with scrapers or old knives. Buckets of water and sponges were used to daub the old paper and people crowded round different bits of the wall to get in on the action. There was an unwritten competition about who could pull the largest strip. They say many hands make light work, but like most old sayings, there were limits to its truth. This tested those limits to the full. Cleaning up after a crowd could be more effort than doing the job in the first place but it kept folk entertained for a day or two. Brian provided the music on his record deck and people brought their favourite 45s to add to the stack. So, to a backing track of *Surfin' USA*, the Ronettes *Be my Baby* and the Beatles *I*

Want to Hold your Hand, the walls were prepared for their new adornment. At least there was no carpet to be bothered about and the furniture, what there was, could be piled up at one end while they worked. Vee was in her element with an open house. Hal, meanwhile, had his pot of tea on the doorstep or in Maggie's. Later, when the real decorating started, he would happily give the benefit of his advice.

'You better check the pattern first, see you've got enough'; 'I'd cut it just about there and use a sharp kitchen knife, it works better than those old scissors'; 'Not too much paste, it will just rip the paper'.

'Hal, will you just shut up? Bugger off to Maggie's or have a bet. Just get out of my way!' Vee didn't mince her words.

Ash was a great help because he was tall and could reach without a chair to stand on. There were no ladders, so chairs and a plank across two of the seats was enough to be getting on with. Geoff was good at pasting using the kitchenette table that had a Formica top. It was primitive but it worked. The hall and stairs proved much more problematic. They were high and had never been decorated. Vee thought just a bit of paint might suffice. Either way, there was the height. Cue Hal with his latest bit of advice. He was no DIY man but he came up with a plan. Ash and he would hold the kitchen table while standing on different stairs. Vee balancing on top would paint. It was precarious to say the least because to get the height they had to hold it quite high at some points. Brian held on to Vee's legs just to steady her. Linda made cups of tea and answered any callers to the door, while the littler ones just sat and laughed. It was like a slapstick pantomime sketch with paint going everywhere.

'Good job we've only got the one girl to get married,' Hal declared. 'Brian, have I ever told you about a place called Gretna Green?'

Vee got to work with bits of Fablon on the leatherette settee. With the few cushions she had spread around, no one would notice. There would be enough glasses with those she'd got from The Peel Hall pub when she worked there; shame if people were that nosy to look at the pub stamp on each one. The men could just drink out of the bottles. She had a few cups and saucers for those who preferred tea. They didn't match, but there would be enough for any hoity toity guests, if they had any, and Flo would always help out.

The wedding rituals began on the Friday before the main ceremony. It was before hen nights and stag dos were so elaborate, at least in our area. But there were still rituals to be considered. The one in Linda's case involved the bride's last day at work. 'Her last day of freedom' it was sometimes called. For Linda, it was a bit unfortunate working at a factory that made curtain tape. The girls covered her coat with odd bits of tape sewn all over, and made a wig like a hat of the same stuff and a big sign about getting married which was attached with string and tinkling bells. Then a whole troupe of them escorted her home, making her get off the bus at an early stop, and slowly parading her through the estate. They made lots of noise, banging things and shouting, and everyone came out cheering. She looked like Worzel Gummidge walking down Ashurst Road with her large noisy, giggling entourage. A girls' night followed from which Ash and the lads were definitely banished. There was chaos in the house the next morning – you couldn't move for hairdressers and make-up boxes, girls laughing hyena-style and nervous men trying to keep out of the way. Flowers started arriving and were duly pinned on everyone. If you stood still, you got a flower pinned to your chest. Vee spent most of the time trying to tidy up after everyone before they left for the church.

Linda wore a ballerina lacy white dress and looked like Tinkerbell without the wings. Hal had a new suit from Mr Potts. Vee wore a ruby red dress, pencil skirt style with a small slit up the leg. It was from the catalogue along with a three-quarter length black and white faux fur coat and a white wide-brimmed hat (Twiggy style) that she borrowed from Margaret Waterfield. But it was Gary who stole the show in his green velvet page-boy outfit, a large frilly ruffle-fronted shirt and home-made buckles on his shiny shoes. They couldn't get buckles anywhere, so Vee improvised with some tin foil and cardboard. He also stole the day at the service, shouting out loud and persistently: 'What number is it, Brian?' as they sang *All Things Bright and Beautiful*. Hal couldn't wait to get to the Benchill Pub for the reception. Not for a drink but to take his teeth out – they were driving him and everybody else mad. He spoke like a radio presenter not quite tuned in, with a whistle between each word. It felt dangerous in his presence because you had that unnerving feeling that at some point soon you would be hit by flying teeth. Thank God for the arrival of the ham salad. He wrapped the dentures in a serviette and Vee secretly transferred them to her white patent leather handbag as she knew by late evening no one would be able to find them. The wedding went well, no surprises, no fights or fall-outs, and even Mary Ellen (and Pa) smiled. Hal cried a bit, though he wouldn't admit to it, and would later blame it on the rum, but everyone knew it was for his little girl.

CHAPTER 7

Mary Ellen behaved herself, like a grand dowager duchess, at the wedding, but she had also managed to keep abreast of all that was happening in recent months at Ashurst Road. She had kept a few spies in the camp, so there was, in truth, little she didn't know about Hal's household and family affairs. She'd persuaded Tommy Rand, the orphan lodger-cum-cake-maker, that Hal and Vee's would be a lovely day out in the country for him, especially on a Sunday when Vee would cook something resembling a Sunday lunch. It was rarely a roast joint and even more rarely a chicken, but perhaps some neck-end chops or a rolled breast of lamb. (Unless Ash had managed to get them something special on the QT.) Tommy came on the bus and invariably outstayed his welcome until late afternoon. Ostensibly, he came to help with the garden, though there was precious little evidence of gardening skills save for the digging of large, deep holes everywhere to bury the builder's rubble and anyone else's rubbish for that matter. Still, he came and gave the kids a sixpence if they were lucky. He liked to play cards while Hal had his afternoon sleep; Whist or Newmarket. He wasn't a great source of information for Mary Ellen, but she gleaned the odd bit of news and the occasional smell of scandal. She noted weak points, arguments with the kids and the like, she knew about future plans and the inevitable money problems. Linda balked at paying rent and board out of her early pay packets. In fact, one notorious night she threw her pay packet across the room at Vee and stormed out. 'You might as well have the bloody lot!' she declared. She returned later, all tears and apologies. Brian, ever the charmer, was always out and about on the street but wanting more stuff to supplement the amp and mic he'd bought from PJ Proby (famous for splitting his trousers on stage) for his new band. These snippets of news in Mary Ellen's hands would prove very useful for her scheming.

Walter (remember, he was Hal's younger brother, the favourite son) was also useful to Mary Ellen now that she had got him a car, though this was temporarily scuppered by that blasted lodger. (Mary Ellen wondered what he was up to taking them out for days to Blackpool. Was Hal with them or was the lodger after Vee?) All these snippets were stored as possibly helpful in the future. Walter, and his wife Lillian, were good for getting the smaller kids on their side. An odd copper here and another there oiled the wheels of possible future division, and division was a pre-requisite for rule. Mary Ellen didn't need Machiavelli to teach her that. Geoff liked to go to Walter and Lillian's house for a sleep-over, at least he did for a while. The tiny terraced house on Peabody Street in Salford had its own strange charm. There was the bizarre green smog in the air with its pungent smell hovering above the canal close by. There were the tiny rooms, cosy in the dark nights. Plus, Geoff was the centre of attention, especially with Lillian, so there was usually a new toy. Most of all, there was the outside loo. Walter and Lillian had managed to get hold of a few carpet sample books which they undid and placed them throughout the backyard like a carpet mat path that led to the loo. Geoff was mesmerised and reported back to Vee,

'Guess what, Mum, they have even got a carpeted backyard!'

Vee looked at the bare asphalt floors in her home with some regret, but she reminded him they did have a bath and a toilet inside their house. He was satisfied and, in the end, always preferred to be home with Gary, Mam and Dad and the kids on the street. But for Mary Ellen, it was another little pinprick in the happy family game in Wythenshawe. It was a situation worth grooming, but for now she accepted it would have little impact. So, she turned on a bit of old-fashioned charm and proposed a family holiday. There had never been one before and she offered to pick up some of the cost. There would be her and Pa, Lou, her sister (widowed, fussy and teary but easily pliable), Tommy Rand would come too and pay for the transport, which was another plus. Would Hal, Vee and the kids like to join? But before that, she played an ace. She didn't ask Hal directly, rather she talked about it with Vee through the kids.

'Wouldn't you like to come to the seaside?' she propositioned. 'There will be donkey rides and playparks and ice-cream galore, and Mum and Dad would play with you all day!'

How could Hal say no to all that and dash the kids' dreams? It would be nice to get away; Vee had never had such a holiday and had been through quite a time. It was planned for the summer so they could start saving. Mary Ellen was painfully thoughtful and she would help out a bit with the cost, she promised, though in the end the bit was a bit. Nevertheless, they all looked forward to it and Mary Ellen went ahead and booked chalets at Pontin's Holiday camp, Heysham Head, Morecombe. Maybe it would keep them going over the winter.

Before that, Christmas loomed. Vee loved Christmas, though not the bills, which sometimes took half the next year to recover from. Gary was easy to please but Geoff, that bit older, was getting more demanding. He wanted a bike. 'Not a hand-me-down!' he explained. 'My own two-wheeled big-boy bike.' That was typical of Geoff – ideas above his station. Vee hoped the clubman, Mr Potts, would oblige, so she promised herself not to get too much from him in the coming months.

Hal had other plans for Geoff.

'I think you are still too small for a big-lad two-wheeled bike,' he told Geoff. 'But never fear, me and John the baker have come up with a plan. Come here a minute and lie down on the floor.'

Geoff, dutiful as ever, obliged. Hal got out a tape measure to size him up. He wrote the length down in a little book and then sucked on the pencil.

'I think we will have to stretch you,' he concluded, 'but not too much, just enough. We had better start tomorrow if you are going to be ready for Christmas.'

So, the ritual of stretching began. John the baker sat on the settee and Hal on his chair while Geoff lay obediently between. Hal held his head and John his feet as they lifted him off the floor and pulled, never too hard but enough for him to feel something might be happening. Then he was measured again in the hope that as the weeks before Christmas passed it would be enough to increase his height to ride a new bike. It didn't work, but fortunately they had a plan B up their sleeves. Wooden blocks were screwed on to the pedals just big enough to make his feet reach. 'The bike will last a bit longer,' said Hal.

Geoff was an easy target for Hal's teasing.

The frozen Christmas turkey was kept in the outhouse to defrost. The door from the kitchen into the outhouse was secured by the rope that was linked to the pully system of the maiden that hung in the kitchen. The maiden was used to dry clothes and then the ironed shirts for the week were hung over each rail for easy access. Hal told Geoff and Gary a long-convoluted tale about how, when he killed a chicken in Heywood Street, he would quickly, with a twist of the wrist, break its neck. They were disgusted. They were even more disgusted when he told them that often the dead chicken would, for some time, still run around the yard with its head hanging loose. They were horrified. 'It's like that sometimes with frozen turkeys,' he continued. 'When they thaw out, they can run around for a while, but it's best just to leave them. That's why we needed a strong rope on the maiden to keep the Christmas turkey in the outhouse just in case, as it thaws, it begins to run around.' That night, as they watched telly, he told Geoff to go and get some coal from the bunker at the far end of the outhouse. Geoff duly got up to go when Harold said quick as a flash, 'Mind – be careful opening the outhouse door just in case the turkey is running around.' Geoff was terrified right until the moment when the turkey was safely in the oven on Christmas Eve.

The blocks were already attached to the bike w Christmas morning, Geoff pulled back the sheet th. was hiding the bike. It was the same year Gary got Escalado, a horse racing board game that he was desperate to get his hands on and force everyone to play – he was the horse racing fanatic of the family, his dad's protégé. Gary loved horses, horse racing and show jumping. Once, he turned the back garden into a complete circuit of jumps and turns. We would take turns running around being timed and scoring faults. Even Hal would have a go when no one was looking.

It was a dry January, not in the alcoholic sense but in the weather one. Geoff learned to ride his spanking new bike with pride. He loved it, apart from the problem of getting on and off. Hal would set him going and he would ride up and down the street until he tired. He was too small to get his feet to the ground without crashing the bike. The other kids would shouted loudly, 'Uncle Hal! Geoff's coming off his bike.' Hal would have to run down the steps to catch him and the bike. That would teach Hal for doing his stretching prank.

It was also the year that Brian started his campaign to get a Lambretta or scooter. Vee was not well pleased. 'Anything *but* a motorbike,' she declared. Usually, especially with Brian, she would do anything to make him happy. This time 'anything' didn't stretch to a motorbike. She was clear and definite. Brian sulked and simmered. He was good at that. His James Dean impression gained him many girl groupies, but his mum stayed firm about the bike. 'No,' was her final statement. She knew that it would end in tears, but little did she understand how that might come about or how final it might feel.

Meanwhile, Linda and Ash, home early from their honeymoon in a caravan in rainy Talacre in Wales, had moved into the back room. A new bed settee took the centre though in reality they would rarely sit in the room as a lounge. Sadly, moving the settee upstairs proved more difficult and while they were busy looking at one end, the other rested on a light bulb and burnt a hole in the leatherette. Linda cried buckets; she seemed all at sea. She was also sick every morning. Vee knew the signs.

Cheryl arrived in the May. A tiny wrinkled, purple prune, though at 6lb 8oz she was bigger than any of Vee's offspring. Her home-coming brought with it a huge crisis. Cheryl certainly wasn't flourishing, far from it. She was a worrying colour, hardly taking milk and had developed a rash. Dr Michael, the local GP, called round after his surgery and with a grave face went to call an ambulance. It arrived quickly with its bell ringing. Linda, still in a dressing gown, left the house with Ash, clutching their tiny bundle. Vee stood at the door of the ambulance and watched as her daughter climbed aboard. 'Linda, get the baby done,' was the advice she bestowed. Linda knew what that meant even if Ash was a little unsure. The dreaded meningitis virus had struck. At the hospital, the chaplain performed an emergency baptism just as Vee had advised. Perhaps more superstition than anything, but Vee just needed to do something. Troubled days and nights followed, but the little one survived. A miracle, well yes, but a medical one first and foremost. Linda and the baby came home in a taxi. Vee got on with another day, thrilled to have her daughter and granddaughter back in the crowded home.

Looking back, it seems life was always precarious and maybe still is for many. Life also seems unfair, but then who is the arbiter of life justice? Those down on their luck rarely get easy pick-you-ups and seem much more likely to face more kicks. That's how Vee saw it anyway. The only practical response was to say, 'What's the bloody use complaining!'

CHAPTER 8

It was an old mini-bus that Tommy Rand had chartered, but it did the job. When it arrived at Ashurst Road it already seemed jam-packed full. There were another two adults and two kids to squash behind the driver, as well as the battered old cases. Brian was coming along after work on the train, already setting a good distance between them all. Hal led the songs with a few rude additions and the kids laughed all the way. As they drove into the old prisoner of war camp, the sun was shining. They were billeted in Row C, Chalet 57. For Vee, Hal and the kids it was funny how the number stuck in their minds so quickly.

Middleton Towers Holiday opened in 1939 and grew to be the largest holiday camp in the Pontin's empire. Holiday camps were popular things in the 50s and 60s with thousands trekking through their doors. 'Holidays for the masses', produced like family boot camps. 'Hi Di Hi' campers boomed from the camp loudspeaker system, waking people up, calling them to meals in the great canteen (cue crashing piles of plates and loud cheers), informing them of all the day's delights: Hunt the Pirate, Bluecoats Entertain, Bingo in the theatre, large four-seater bikes to pedal around the site, sandcastle competition, donkey racing and the nightly show. This, and more, were open to all campers.

WHO IS JOE DANIELS? DOES IT MATTER?

At the centre of the park was the SS Berengaria, an art deco building in the shape of a (concrete) cruise liner. It contained a theatre and a dance hall, a one-armed bandit hall, and a coffee-cum-gift shop. Near to the ship there was a swimming pool and some huts with bikes, crazy golf and a proper roller-skater rink. The Kids' Club happened on the 'ship' but first the Bluecoats processed the camp like pied pipers, collecting the kids in one long conga line. Aunt Lou and Tommy Rand spent most of the time on the slot machines. Hal did at first but got barred because he won too much on the OXO machine! He shared his winnings with the kids who promptly poured the pennies into 'losing machines', but they laughed and laughed. The sun was kind to them and memories were of a bright, warm sun-kissed holiday. There was a backing track of the Supremes' *Baby Love*, Herman's Hermits *Something tells me something's going to happen tonight*, *Ferry cross the Mersey* with Gerry and the Pacemakers, and Freddy and the Dreamers singing *You were made for me*, which Geoff did a squeaky impersonation of in the talent competition. Linda visited one day with the baby, the day Vee won the glamorous granny competition (she was only thirty-five after all). Gary stole the show as the curly-headed Tarzan, complete with gravy browning for a good tan. Amid all this, Brian simmered like James Dean in *Rebel without a Cause*, his favourite film. He would stand sneering near the juke box while a constant crowd of mini-skirted girls surrounded him. He said he hated the camp and the holiday, but there were obviously some attractions. The week passed quickly and even Aunt Lou seemed to enjoy herself. For years after, Gary could impersonate the loudspeaker announcements and remembered C57, the chalet.

It was probably at the camp, on that almost perfect holiday, that a different plan was hatched. Mary Ellen watched the disaffected Brian with interest. She had given him a bit of extra cash, and now she got young Walter to speak to him with a proposition. The scooter! She wouldn't buy one for him but perhaps she'd help with a down payment. She agreed to stand guarantor, too. Brian was delirious and didn't even begin to consider the consequences. In a couple of weeks, he arrived in Ashurst Road with his Lambretta. All hell let loose.

It was too late to take away the bike, Vee accepted that, but it didn't take away the fear every time he left the house. Neither did his delight in his bike take away the seething anger. Vee rarely lost her temper. Over the years she had pushed herself against many odds, pushed and pushed. She had bitten her lip, tried to keep the peace, bounced back and tried to rise above the family games of control that Hal's mother had not only contributed to but, in the main, had orchestrated. There was no calm left in her, just anger. This time it was Hal who was trying to pacify her, not the other way around. But his heart was never in it. The goodwill promoted by the Pontin's effect disappeared the minute Vee and Hal had it confirmed that it was Mary Ellen who had facilitated the bike purchase against everything that Vee had said and wanted. Mary Ellen had blatantly and cruelly attacked Vee's motherhood. There would be no turning back.

Hal took charge and it was simple, straightforward and fatal. He went to see his mother for what seemed like one last time. He played it straight and cool. He laid out the situation and, as Mary Ellen started one of her histrionic vocal shudders, he stopped her in her tracks.

'You better listen to this, Mum, and listen hard,' he said firmly with some simmering anger. 'This is finally it. I want nothing more to do with you, with Walter or John. Stay away from my family. You will not be welcomed. That's it, over and done.' With that, he left a silenced and stupefied Mary Ellen, and a stunned Heywood Street. He vowed not to return and he never did.

Brian, in the meantime, realised he had overstepped the mark. He loved the bike, but he loved his mum more. He was traumatised out of his sultry adolescent moods; it was time to grow up, and in reality, the worst a lad like him could witness was his mum in tears, tears of anger and fear.

In a sense, nothing else changed except that the seeds of a major change were sown in quite a different way than anyone could have expected or foreseen. Vee knew from the tea leaves that predicting what might happen was a difficult and dangerous affair. She never felt she could rest easy. If it wasn't Mary Ellen at her heels, it would be something else. Looking right, it hit you on the left. Offer one cheek and it would take the other too.

On the arrival of Amanda, Linda and Ash's second baby, the council offered them a flat of their own, not far away in Adensfield Drive. Like Darnbrook Drive for Vee, Linda's first home was small but adequate. History just repeating itself. There was at least a welcome bit of breathing space in Ashurst Road though she had to help Linda put the home together. Linda's bottom drawer was full with chip pans, cruet sets, towels and little bits of Tupperware and silly knick-knacks, but there was quite a bit missing. Of course, she had the bed settee with its patched hole on the side. Thank God for sticky plastic. Anyway, Geoff and Gary could move into the backroom and Brian would get the bunkroom. She and Hal might just have their own room for once in a very long while.

Family life continued full pelt and for a while Hal was at his best. Meal times in the Miller household were not often family events. Rarely did they all even eat the same food. There were the kids who needed feeding early, Brian when he came in from work later, and then Hal, who liked a new potato rather than chips. One notorious whole family meal was interrupted when Geoff, in full finicky mode, complained that his fork hadn't been washed properly. Hal stopped the meal and, with a serious face, made Geoff show his fork to the assembled table. It wasn't acceptable to have a dirty fork, he told everyone. 'Who washed these dishes?' he asked. Vee held up her guilty hands. 'Well, Vee, it just isn't good enough. I think Geoff better see to all the dishwashing for the next couple of weeks so we don't have that problem again.' Pernickety Geoff learned his lesson and never made that mistake again. He soon knew that you could get away with most things, say almost anything as long as you respected your mum. That was the golden rule of the house. That and going to the bedroom if ever you 'had monk on'. Hal had suffered enough of that in Heywood Street.

The next few months belonged to Brian. He soon tired of the bike, fortunately without an accident – *thank God*, thought Vee. His itchy feet resulted in him and his mates making hairbrained schemes to emigrate to Australia or South Africa, or just somewhere where he would become famous and rich. Eventually, he settled on a summer job in Guernsey. Giving up his job at the photographic shop in town, he and two of his mates headed into the sun. A few weeks later, they headed back again. It was a disaster. He got a job at the Co-op dairy and sulked. Amid all this, he had 'sold' his bike to a mate, Alan Ramsbottom. (Alan was the one who got so drunk one night he fell asleep on our toilet.) He didn't sell it 'properly' but for a bit of cash-in-hand (for the Guernsey trip) which they'd agreed would be made up in in taking on the HP payments. However, 'Ramsy' – or sometimes 'Arsy' – disappeared, Brian thought to South Africa. So did the bike (not sure where to) with the payment book (he hadn't made any payments).

It was a Sunday afternoon when Walter turned up in his car. Sheepishly, he knocked on the door and was invited in. Vee got Hal out of bed (his afternoon sleep interrupted) and made a pot of tea. She had a feeling they would need it. Walter was all coy and obsequious but eventually got to the point.

'It's about the bike,' he said. 'Mum regrets she ever got involved in the whole business, she just wanted to please Brian. She is so sorry about all the fuss it caused.'

Hal listened without saying a word. Walter was on the backfoot, especially when no response was forthcoming. He feared Hal's temper and his fists.

'It's just that Brian has defaulted on the payments and mum has had debt collectors calling, wanting to cash in the guarantee she made. It's a lot of money for her on the old age pension.'

Hal tried not to smirk too obviously as he glanced at Vee. This was a moment, a real moment. 'That's really bad news,' he said calmly. 'I hope she will manage. I'll tell Brian the situation when I next see him. He's working in Guernsey at the moment. It's a summer job. I'm afraid I don't even have an address I can give you.'

Walter stuttered over his tea cup.

'We was just wondering whether you and Vee could help out? After all, he's your son.' Walter knew that he was crossing a line. Now his adrenaline levels started to rise as Hal grew red at the gills. Vee interrupted.

'Please tell her we'd love to help, we really would, Walter, but sadly it's way beyond our means. We are struggling most weeks to make ends meet. We have the little ones to think of. And to be perfectly honest, there's only one person to blame.'

Walter left not best suited, but I think he was glad to get out without being thrown out, literally. 'Some things come home to roost,' Hal declared. Vee just said, 'Best to be patient and polite, Hal. She will get the point.' Hopefully she did. The bike was never mentioned again. Well, at least not on Ashurst Road.

Soon Brian had a new ruse. Thinking back, he *was* talented and handsome but a bit flaky. He still wanted to travel the world, but how would he pay? Certainly not with the dairy factory wage. He would join the forces, the mechanics section of the RAF. They would teach him to drive. In no time, he had signed up and got a date to start the training. Hal told him that there was no coming back, he had to finish the training, or it would cost him to get out. Brian said he was sure about his decision, but at the same time he was also madly in love with beautiful Marissa Hadfield from Meliden Crescent. He got engaged to Marissa (her exotic name came from her father's time in Italy on his National Service) and her mum visited Vee to talk about wedding plans. She arrived with a sherry bottle in her bag. Meanwhile, Brian went off to RAF Leeming (or was it Halton?) for boot camp.

It was meant to be a simple wedding; Vee and Hal decided to stay quiet and, at least at the outset, expected Marissa's family to pay the bulk of the costs, as was tradition. It didn't all work that way in the end, but it was at least a good opening gambit. This time they would get married at the church hall, newly licensed as a Conventional District Worship Centre – whatever that was. The vicar seemed pleased. The reception was held at the Royal Green pub out near the Parkway. There was a buffet rather than a sit-down meal. Brian, of course, wore his dress blues, Hal had a suit and Vee mustered something together. The kids wore their Whit clothes, each with a new shirt and ties on elastic. Hal was determined not to spend too much, so when Vee said he needed some new shoes, he balked. 'They'll clean up,' he protested. 'No one looks at the dad's shoes,' he said. 'I do,' said Vee. 'When they are yours. You are not showing me up.'

The next week, when she was at the Civic Centre, she had a quick look in Barratt's. She had learned from Hal to stash a little money away, the odd win on the Bingo, the change she collected, and on one or two occasions Hal had forgotten to ask for the day's wage off Mrs Meredith. The Diazepam effect, no doubt! She had enough to buy him a pair of shoes which she duly did. 'Here,' she told him that evening, proudly offering the shiny shoes. 'I saw these in Barratt's and they were a really good deal, so I bought them for you.' 'How much were they?' he asked. She quickly halved the price. 'A really cheap deal – they were just £4.99.' He tried them on and they fit. He got a ten pound out of his wallet and gave it to her. 'That was a good deal. Could you get me another pair to keep as best?' Did he know? Possibly, probably, almost definitely! Whatever, he as always ended up the winner and Vee lost a good bit of her secret cash. That's life! Well, that's life at the Miller's.

The wedding went off well. Hal got stung for at least half of the reception, but by that time, it wasn't worth arguing. It was okay at the reception, though Marissa's mum got a little drunk and flirted with an embarrassed Uncle Reg. Flo sorted it out quickly and firmly. They laughed about it for weeks afterwards. The Millers and the Bakers were not really drinkers or flirters for that matter.

In no time, Brian's travelling bug was to be fulfilled. He, with his new wife, were to be posted to Changi, Singapore.

CHAPTER 9

On the first Sunday of each month, the Church Lads' Brigade bugle band marched around the estate for Parade Sunday. They were attached to the Anglican Mission Hall called All Saints. Geoff was enthralled, mind you, and so were a good number of his pals. They turned up one Monday night and were duly enrolled. Gym classes and military maze-marching, craft work and uniforms. They got stuck in. Geoff was small and light enough to climb and stand atop the human pyramid on display nights, though it always looked a bit shaky to Vee watching from the bottom. Soon Gary was also old enough to join and, as usual, followed his brother but, as always, in his own style. Brigade Camp meant a holiday for both lads which, unbeknown to them, was paid for quietly by one of the leaders. Windermere and Cleethorpes were the two most remembered, Windermere because it was the first and under canvas. Cleethorpes was in a YMCA camp centre with its own sports hall and outdoor swimming pool. (The latter was too cold to use.) At Cleethorpes, Gary and Geoff were put on 'jankers' with their little crowd for arriving back late for tea, their task being to peel big bags of potatoes.

They loved it! Mainly because their captain, Mr Heath, made it fun. He looked after his lads. On the last Friday, there was a trip to the seaside and Mr Heath opened his large sweet jar full of the coppers that he had saved throughout the year. Together, the excited little huddle of lads counted them and divided them. It paid for ice cream, sweets and a few rides at the fun fair. It also meant they had some money to buy presents for everyone at home. Vee kept all those presents in her china cabinet. A plastic cruet set, a pot shire horse, a nick-knack with 'Cleethorpes' emblazoned on the side. To her, these were real treasures, not tat. At least one (that gold-covered plastic cruet set) had cost more than pocket money – a whole evening's potato peeling!

Every year, the Brigade had a day at Bell Vue Zoo in Gorton near the centre of Manchester. It wasn't much of a zoo, but it had fairground rides, and the Speedway Stadium (home of the Belle Vue Aces and the Colts) made it a great place for the marching and displays. It was one of the highlights of their year and Gary and Geoff persuaded Hal and Vee to go and watch them in the march past, the athletics display and Geoff in his starring role: topping the human pyramid. After the tattoo in the morning, there was a grand picnic and then everybody was free to visit the animals, or more likely to go on the rides. Hal and Gary loved the more daring rides. They only liked the dodgems if you could crash into everyone, the Waltzers if the lad would spin you round even faster, the Ferris wheel if you could swing the seat, and the log flume if it was high, fast and wet. Most of all, they needed Geoff and Vee to be with them so that they could frighten them on each ride. Vee sometimes could just barely watch from below or the side, and Geoff only agreed to join them so as not to be a complete wet rag. It wasn't fun unless there was a scream and a white ashen face of terror to stare and cause a laugh. Geoff usually obliged; he was the wimp, preferring really to walk around and just look at things in amazement or, occasionally, daringly 'hook a duck'! Vee would have preferred the Bingo but it didn't matter as the prizes weren't that good.

Something happened in the Speedway Stadium that changed things for everyone. It was quite an innocent remark but its impact was long term and drastic. Vee found herself sitting next to another Mrs Miller, whose husband was one of the Brigade leaders. Innocently, Vee remarked, 'Aren't they girls in uniform marching in fancy patterns, over there across the stadium's central field?'

'Of course,' came the reply. 'That's the Church Girls' Brigade. Sadly, we haven't got one of them at our church.'

'Well, we ought to have,' feisty Vee replied. 'That would be only fair.'

That was the end of the comments, but not the end of the conversation. The next week, Vee had a visit from the vicar, well, in reality, the curate, but never mind. 'Mrs Miller, I was just calling round to say hello and because someone told me that you might be interested in starting a Church Girl's Brigade at our church.'

Vee was stopped in her tracks, somewhat paralysed for words and desperately trying to stay polite, but she knew she was trapped. So it was that Vee was initiated as the Captain of the CGB. She got Margaret Waterfield to help her and young Ann, Janice's older sister. There were training sessions and uniforms, and she managed to get the kids in the street to tout all their friends. Within a few months, they were up and running. Marching up and down the hall, keep-fit for girls with ribbons and flags, crafts and badges. It was an instant success. Vee realised as Parade Sunday approached that if the girls had to go to church, so did she. It wasn't as bad as she thought. Though there were few folks from the council estate who attended – most came from the private houses – she was made welcome.

Hal thought it was hilarious. Her hat with its red and white plume, and the red lanyard on her shoulder, he said, was bad enough – all she needed was a tambourine and she could join the Sally Army. Much teasing and mocking followed, but 'he who mocks most is usually heading for a leap (or a fall) of some kind.' Vee told him that the Church Men's Society was having a darts competition and wondered if Hal was up for taking part. He couldn't say no, and after all, it was only a game of darts. That game of darts, which, by the way, he won, changed his life.

The tenacious young vicar/curate asked Hal about helping him out. It started with cleaning the windows and Hal got some of the toe-rags on the estate to help him. He was a bit of a local hero; he helped set up the Christmas Fayre, supported Vee with the girls' group and then started helping the curate set up each week for the Sunday Service. He took it really seriously, almost measuring each cushion into place. Everybody in the family, and others, were dragooned into helping. Then, miracle of all miracles, he actually attended church with Vee. He felt like a fish out of water, but he went.

It was a new world to navigate, but at heart what made

them continue was that here they were respected. The curate was wise enough to see them as useful gatekeepers to the council estate. The estate was a hard nut to crack in church mission terms. It was then; but it's even harder now. The Church Girls' Brigade grew in each age group and in no time at all, it was the largest brigade group in the local battalion. For Vee, it was the girls that mattered. She not only cared about them, but she had had her own personal experiences, good and bad, and they helped her understand the girls and how to connect with them. For years to come, many would come to her for a chat. A chat about their children, and in some cases, their grandchildren. She knew their mums, their dads, and in short, she was one of them.

This entry into church wasn't without its difficulties. The church on the whole welcomed them with open arms, but it had its own practice of what Geoff would later term 'cultural circumcision'; church folk didn't swear (difficult for Hal), rarely smoked (impossible for them both), had matching cups and saucers when people called for a cup of tea (Vee had a couple with chips and they didn't match), generally had quite posh houses – carpet and nice furniture, phones and tuneful doorbells (the Millers had none of these trappings). Most of the churchwomen arranged flowers, baked lovely cakes, sorted out their matching hats, met for coffee and occasionally (very occasionally) dusted the altar. After all, most employed cleaners at their homes and rarely picked up an iron, never mind a decorating brush. Vee cleaned – that was her main work. She didn't particularly like doing it but she could do it. Now she was learning there were other things that she could do that they couldn't. She could organise a girls' group that grew and grew and grew. People liked her, they liked talking to her. Vee hated what she called the 'Tupperware stuff' that made life tick in the church. 'It's about time that lot learned about real life,' she would comment.

The curate's wife lived up to her name: Joy. She was gentle, kind, very earnest and keen to get to know Vee. 'I'm having a Tupperware party at the vicarage, Mrs Miller. It's to raise money for new altar linen. Could you come? You would enjoy it, I'm sure.'

Vee was quite sure she wouldn't. She knew she would feel like a fish riding a bike. Most of all, she knew she would come back with a Tupperware box set that she didn't want, and didn't need, which would cost her an arm and a leg. But she went, just to please Joy, her new friend. That challenge was easier than the next. The vicar was keen to get more representative lay folk involved in the services. The headteacher was a *Reader* and there were others who read lessons. They were all posh, though ever so polite.

'I was hoping you might read *The Comfortable Words* for us in church next week, Vera.' She panicked, but he showed her the bit in the service and let her take a book home to have a read through. She practised and practised. In fact, we all had a go. No one was really sure what some of the words meant, never mind how to pronounce them. That was especially true of the word 'propitiation'. A technical word for appeasing an angry God. Not many of the regular congregants (in fact, not all clergy) could have explained it, but Cranmer had deemed that it should be read out each week before the confession and the

1928 Prayer Book kept it. We all tried different pronunciations, but Vee didn't have the luxury of waiting to hear how others pronounced it in church. She was reading it next Sunday. Vee's perceived problem was that, however she tried, it had 'piss' in the middle. Surely she couldn't say 'piss' in church? But she, or we, couldn't think of any other option. She put on her brave face and spoke with her Sunday voice and somehow nobody bothered. Perhaps they didn't hear her or were too polite to say anything. For a while she tried to avoid the vicar and his wife so that there were no more requests that gave her a headache, though she did put him on the spot at a later date and asked him to explain what it meant. She suggested that she take him (and Joy) to the Mecca Bingo Hall and see how they felt, an idea that Geoff resurrected years later when training ordinands.

Meanwhile, Hal got more involved. He even joined the vicar some days for Morning Prayer. It gave him a structure and a purpose. The vicar talked to him like a human being, he asked his advice about how to deal with the teenagers who hung around the church doors of a night. He was interested in Hal's life. He liked to get Hal talking about his days growing up, the boxing and the various jobs he'd had. He was fascinated with the chimney sweeping. Hal often became his interpreter for what was going on in the lives of people on the council estate. What the vicar saw as the devil at work, Hal saw as debt, debt collectors and real poverty. What the vicar thought might be depravity, Hal explained was deprivation and survival. They became friends in their own sort of way.

'Harold, I have this idea,' the vicar said one morning. 'I

wondered if you would become my Honorary Verger at the church? I'm afraid it is a voluntary post, but it would help me to have someone at my side getting things ready, clearing up and the like. For a funeral or a wedding there would be some expenses. Have a think about it.'

It wasn't the greatest of opportunities, but to Hal it was a huge boost in confidence. It had been a long time since he felt so valued. He agreed, and as we all learned he took the job very seriously.

*

For both Vee and Hal, slowly, almost without noticing, faith became part of their lives, a living thing. What started as attending church reluctantly became deeply moving, even life-changing. It was hard to articulate but they both became valued members of their new community. They exuded a basic, primitive wisdom, or perhaps they just exuded street nous which is not normally in great supply in church communities. Even God got a way in. Vee first, and then Hal went on the parish retreat. The women went to a convent in Horbury. It was a supposedly a silent weekend. On the whole, they kept the rule but Vee and Margaret Waterfield talked in the gardens and smoked out of the window of their rooms. Hal went with the men to Mirfield. Comparing notes later, the men got the better deal. The monks liked their food, unlike the Sisters at Horbury who seemed a little more frugal. Also, there was a good pub in the village of Mirfield that the men (and some of the monks) went to on the Friday night before they went into silence. I wouldn't say Hal and Vee had found religion, but it had found them.

CHAPTER 10

In spring 1968, there was another visit from Hal's brothers, both of them this time. They probably needed each other for moral support or safety. They had not met the newly forged Hal and Vee. This time, their visit placed Hal and Vee in a dilemma. Pa had died and Mary Ellen wanted Hal to know. Hal had little against the gentle but weak Pa whom he had for so long believed was his father. Would Hal visit the old woman? Would he come to the funeral, please, they begged? Hal said he would think about it but couldn't promise anything. They finished their cups of tea and left. Their presence hung in the air. Hal was unsure whether this was another ruse from Mary Ellen. He wondered if he was being reeled in again. Vee kept quiet. Her stomach said everything she needed to say but she refused to interfere. She, too, held an affection for Pa, who wouldn't hurt a fly, though neither would he stand up for himself. Apparently, the house in Heywood Street was no longer the centre of the empire. Heywood Street (renamed at some point, for some obscure reason, Harpenden Street) had been demolished as part of slum clearance. Mary Ellen and Pa had moved to a flat in a tower block on the Darnhill Estate in Heywood over in Lancashire.

Hal decided to visit. He would take Geoff and Gary, and then Vee agreed reluctantly to go along. Vee dreaded the visit with all her being. On the journey there, she felt her whole stomach being pulled in different directions, squashed and twisted so that it was like a dead weight deep inside her. But she was determined not to be cowed again, to maintain her dignity and to see it through. She did just that, but was helped by just seeing Mary Ellen. She not only looked old, she *was* old, a pathetic old lady. Perhaps Vee had grown up at last. Whatever Mary Ellen had done in the past, she had lost her spell and her power. She was in her place and there she would stay. For Hal, the old spell she had spun was also broken. He had little she could take from him now. He and Vee had survived and had what they needed, little enough as it was. Mary Ellen had little to offer him, except perhaps for one thing. The very thing she would never volunteer: the truth about his real dad. The truth about Joe Daniels. They went back to Darnhill for Pa's funeral at the crematorium in Oldham. He and Vee shed a tear but, in all honesty, they struggled to find any depth of compassion for Mary Ellen. She had drained them both of any emotion except the ability to despise. That wasn't very pretty and they recognised it. Now Walter, her favourite, and John, the younger son (along with his eight children) would have to bear responsibility for her care. It was probably the last time they saw her. On the way home, they took the first bus into Manchester town centre and instead of then getting the second (the 165 to Peel Hall) straight away, the four of them went to a restaurant for a meal. It was the first time they had ever done that and Hal had steak and chips and Vee some plaice. It was a little bit celebratory and a little bit relief. They hadn't won, but it was over. They had laid the past to rest.

By pure chance in Hal's dealings over Pa's funeral, one new snippet of evidence about his biological dad dropped into Hal's lap. He saw for the first time Mary Ellen and Walter's marriage certificate. It was a just a quick glance, but something struck him. Mary Ellen also had another name. Afterwards, Ash helped him get a copy from the archives and records office. It was a strange affair; Mary Ellen's marriage name was Daniels or Karavitch. Could this be the missing link – was Joe Daniels called Karavitch? Each revelation seemed to produce only more questions. His yearning for the truth was a quest that had too many twists and turns for any peaceful resolution. Ash tried to help. They found a few Karavitches in Miles Platting and Cheetham Hill, which was not so far away. They all belonged to the Jewish community, and were tailors by trade. But there was no Joe (or Joseph) among them.

Ash scoured the area for clues. One Karavitch had a take-away food business. Ash said he was the spitting image of Hal, but he would not speak to them – in fact, he asked them to leave his shop. Another dead end?

Meanwhile, Geoff couldn't be prouder of his dad who became more and more a leader in the local church. He was particularly pleased by his honorary role and title as verger, a pleasure that was particularly helpful when Geoff began at the big new school. When school term started, along with the rest of the registration class, he had to fill in that annual form that was given out in the first week at school: name, address, parents' names and jobs, and emergency contacts. Importantly for Geoff, for once, he wouldn't have to write 'on the sick' next to his dad's job. So, he wrote that Hal 'worked' at the church. He filled it in quickly and neatly, and then sat back. His teacher, Mr Harrison, a big bear of a man who majored in woodwork, called him to the front.

'Miller, I don't know your dad, but he definitely isn't that,' he said. 'Take this home and show him.'

Geoff was indignant and humiliated. How dare he question what his dad did! Just wait 'til he told Hal! His dad would be down here like a shot. Mr Harrison didn't know what was coming to him.

He arrived home in high drama, told the story and gave his dad the folded sheet. Hal looked at it and showed it straight to Vee.

'Sorry, son, but your teacher is right. I am definitely not that.'

Geoff had written that his dad was the Church virgin – not verger. Hal explained and fortunately Geoff understood enough to see the funny side.

*

Geoff's secondary school career had had a bit of a wobbly start and I don't mean the registration form boo-boo. His year was the first intake to be introduced to the comprehensive education system in Manchester. Administrative confusion meant that his school allocation hiccupped and he was late getting his place confirmed. The wobble or shaky start was multi-faceted. First, there was getting the uniform. There were free school uniforms for kids whose parents were on benefits. You had to get it from John Lewis, the big and rather upmarket department store in the city centre. All good so far. However, as you would expect, there was no money exchanging hands. A note arrived to take to the store. At the store office on the third floor, you had to collect a small pile of tickets which were used in the right department along with an official uniform list. There were separate queues for the free uniform 'customers' and, of course, no variation or choice. The cap was on the list, so you had to get it but the voucher couldn't be exchanged for an extra tie or shirt. As they found out, there were always ways to remind you that were on 'the benefits'. Geoff's school pals who were not on 'benefits' skipped the queues and Vee and Geoff hated it, but needs must. They got what was needed and allowed, including the dreaded cap which would barely last the first day. Then they treated themselves to a frothy coffee at the Italian café in St Anne's Square.

When Geoff arrived at school, he was placed in the bottom class (1X12) of the streamed intake. He was used to being at the top! Geoff was mortified though he certainly learned some life lessons. He had to persuade the teacher that he could read and write already and do it without appearing to brag in front of his classmates. It took the first half-term for him to be reassessed. Once they realised that he didn't need to learn to read, they knew something was wrong. By Christmas, he was in the top stream. He had moved from 1X12 to 1X1 but had some catching up to do.

Then he hated lunchtimes. It wasn't about friendship groups. He was small and not a fighter, but all the other kids from the street hung out with him, and he was popular. However, free dinner kids queued separately, so he had to leave his mates and join the queue on the right-hand side. This was overseen by the dreaded Mr Ashton, head of metalwork.

He was handy with the strap and ruled the kids with fear and dread. Also, he was never very keen on free dinner kids – "scroungers" he called them. "They should be quiet and grateful." He berated them for not washing their hands properly, not having proper table manners, and not being grateful enough. Geoff panicked when asked to get the tureens for his table – what were tureens, where did he get them? He was lost. Then, to top it all, he was put on Ozzy Osborne's table. Ozzy (not related to the popstar but could well have been) was notorious. He drank the water direct from the jug and dished out the food sparingly for everyone except his friends.

Geoff came home in tears.

However, things improved and not just with his meteoric rise through the streamed classes. Even more helpful was finding out that Ozzy Osborne was one of Mrs Osborne's sons; Vee walked to work with her every morning. A quiet word changed lunchtimes and Ozzy became Geoff's minder. This meant Geoff not only got fed but even had a glass of water. That and the fact that the dreaded cap, the only one that was ever seen, disappeared forever after it supported an ad hoc game of football (or was it hatball?).

In a single moment, a few weeks later, Gary became the centre of attention. Vee blamed the ice cream van but who knows the truth? As Gary ran home across the road with his 99 in hand, he collided with an old van driven by a lad from Glenby Avenue. It was fortunately going reasonably slowly in the opposite direction. An emergency ambulance whisked Gary and Vee to the hospital, and everyone held their breath.

A fractured skull, a black eye and some concussion guaranteed Gary lots of chocolate and sweets for the next few weeks as he recovered. He thought it was *almost* (emphasis on the *almost*) worth it.

The vicar called to visit him, and caught some of Vee's anxiety and anger. With some growing wisdom, he suggested that this might be the moment to do something with all that anger and worry. He helped Vee and the other women begin a campaign for some safe children's facilities on the estate. By now the farm was derelict and would make a perfect site for a park. Vee and her friends went from door to door, collecting signatures to present to the council. The new Lord Mayor lived in the private houses and the vicar was his chaplain; Vera could make a thing of giving him the petition. Then the vicar came to say that Look North (the local ITV station) wanted to film her doing it. Could she get some others to join her? They could do it on the bridge at the centre of the old farm. The vicar would get Councillor Ritchie to come and he would arrange the TV crew. The vicar was really the fixer, Vee the voice of the people. Vee the mother, Vee the girls' group organiser, Vee the church woman, Vee the fresh, naïve but feisty activist. She was interviewed on the evening news, much to the street's delight. A five-minute local hero! This was church mission and community organising 1960's style. The naïve vicar had unleashed the lioness' spirit and learned that children were the quickest way to a mother's heart.

Geoff paved the way for Gary at school, but Gary was always a different beast, his own person. He made his own mark and had much more of Hal's fighting spirit about him, though to be fair he stayed out of most conflicts. The kids were by now good at amusing themselves and the street was really their playground. The council wheels turned slowly in providing that much needed park but it eventually happened long after Geoff, Gary and their contemporaries needed (or could use) it.

*

On Saturdays, it became the craze for all the kids on the street to go to the Tatton Cinema in Gatley, an urban village a good couple of miles walk from their street. They started by going to the Saturday morning club where, for 1/6d they could watch old movie shorts such as the *Lone Ranger*, *Flash Gordon* and the *Dead-End Street Gang*, or cartoons such as *Roadrunner* and *Tom and Jerry*. Soon they progressed to the afternoon matinee (cost 2/3d) with blockbusters such as *That Riviera Touch* with Morecombe and Wise, *Carry on Doctor*, *Those Magnificent Men in their Flying Machines*, or *Monte Carlo or Bust*. For an extra 3d they could buy sweets, though best to get them at the sweet shop next door as the kiosk was too expensive and they didn't have the same choice. At first, they shared everything. You would take a bite of the liquorice stick and pass it on down the line. But some nicked the best bits, like the red sugar-coated tip of the liquorice pipe, or took very large bites. The finishing touch came when Jimmy Etchells, who didn't have sweet money, passed his cold toast up the row, complete with a thick coating of brown sauce. They decided it was better to stick with their own sweets and give Jimmy a share of what they had. It was never simple because no matter where Gary was sitting in the row, he always wanted to eat his sweets in the same order that Geoff did.

'What you having next, Geoff?'

'The torpedoes and the sherbet.'

'Ssh, you two, we're missing the film!'

If anyone had any money left, we would get eight penneth of chips from the chippy to eat on the walk home. Halcyon days!

Kids seemed so much freer then. No doubt there were as many dangers but perhaps we were just naïve. Life was spent in groups that weren't really gangs like the pejorative word implies in today's society, but provided a mixed age security and solidarity. It felt like people looked out for each other. But perhaps memories are always rose-tinted. As they say, 'These are the good old days, just you wait and see.'

The good old days, however, pass quickly even though they are remembered with pleasure.

CHAPTER 11

Valerie, a teenager, was Jud's daughter from a previous relationship. I suppose today we might suggest she had some kind of learning disability. She was also overweight and often unkempt. She didn't have much going for her. She had moved to Wythenshawe from London to be with her dad, straight into Maggie's. For all intents and purposes, she became a kind of errand girl, sent here and there at Maggie's behest and sometimes at everyone else's. Vee felt sorry for her and tried to offer her some kindness.

'Why don't you come over when Linda's here and we can all do our hair together?'

Maggie would never question a suggestion by Vee and as long as Vee could put up with the poor personal hygiene, Valerie was given some respite and experienced some motherly care. She came across regularly for a cup of tea, for a chat and some girly talk. Then she would return to Maggie's where she wasn't treated particularly cruelly, not even unkindly, just overlooked and sent on errands, lots of errands.

We knew that something was up when Valerie began one of her rounds of door knocking. 'Just be patient, she'll get to us eventually!' Hal said as we watched her go from door to door. And sure enough, she did …

On Thursdays, usually it was a little note which said something like: 'Mam said has the master got any coppers he could let her have until next week?'

Or on Tuesdays: 'Mam says would you give Mr Potts a call and say he'll have to miss us this week. We will try and give him double next week.'

Or other days: 'Mam says she has a bale of towels to sell. Would you be interested in them?'

Her request this time was different from the others to say the least.

'Me mam's doing some cleaning and wondered if you had any old wallpaper for the cupboard shelves?'

Vee was open-mouthed. Maggie *cleaning?* That would be a first! Best to help out if possible. Valerie left armed with a few spare rolls, bedroom, lounge and kitchen paper – a good mix. It was the next week when the news broke: her eldest daughter, Bernie, was coming home for Christmas. She had been posted, with her military husband, to some exotic, faraway place – Germany, if I remember correctly – and while there, had given birth to her first child. A first grandchild for Maggie. The whole street was invited to the welcome home party.

The great date arrived and we assembled for the surprise welcome in the parlour. As the lights were turned on, amid the hurrahs there were titters as we all spotted strips of wallpaper from our own homes on the walls around us! Two strips of lounge paper from our house right next to three strips from the Waterfield's kitchen, and then some from the Arkwright's front bedroom. And so on, right round the room. Soon the party got in full swing, the women cooing over the new baby, the men opening their bottles of beer and the kids (lots of them) running around causing havoc. It felt like Christmas had come a few weeks early. It was a night to go down in the legends of Ashurst Road, talked about for years to come.

It was a conversation before school during the following week that changed our minds about that night. We laughed around the toast in the kitchen about the inadequate preparations the dysfunctional family had made for the arrival of Veronica and the baby. We were chided by 'our mam' (a wise old bird if ever there was one) who simply said to us that their preparations might, in our terms, be pathetic and laughable, but at least they had made the effort. You shouldn't decry the energy and the love they displayed. If Bernie and the neighbours knew anything at the end of the party, they knew that Maggie and her family wanted them to know just how important they were to them. Where's the sin in that? We were stopped in our tracks. Of course, it remained funny but ...

Perhaps Vee had Brian and Marissa on her mind. One day soon, they would be returning home to Manchester too. They would bring a new addition to the family in the shape of a bubbly, gurgling Malaysian-speaking infant son (Dean) who had been born in Changi two years ago. He wouldn't really speak Malaysian, Vee had been assured, but the amma who looked after him had spoken only local languages to him and he seemed to respond. Vee couldn't wait to meet the little one and she wanted to make them welcome. Though to be honest, she wasn't thinking of copying Maggie's example.

Whitsun was a big festival in Manchester then. Its origins, apart from its ecclesiological roots, were fairly sectarian. At least they were sectarian in practice. Vee explained that when she was a girl, the Protestants marched through the streets on Whit Sunday into the town centre for a big jamboree. Those who had been confirmed that year held the cords to their local church banner. The girls were dressed in white and wore simple veils. Everybody got new clothes and the little ones walked behind the bands while holding a long rope with all the Sunday School kids. On Whit Mondays, the Catholics walked similar routes straight into Piccadilly Gardens where they had a big service. Same idea, two different communities. Of course, they sang different hymns; the Catholics preferred *Land of the Fathers*, and the Protestants were more likely to sing *Onward Christian Soldiers*. Vee said it usually rained on Whit Monday – or at least the Protestants hoped it did.

The young vicar of Peel Hall was determined to keep the tradition but also to change things. He got on well with Father St John (the Roman Catholic priest) as well as the Methodist minister. He proposed a joint walk through the parish, all together singing each other's hymns after a short service. The Brigade Band would lead the processions. Of course, there were in each community detractors, but most people thought it was a great idea. Vee was convinced and she convinced others.

To be really honest, the kids loved Whitsun but not for the walks or the church celebrations. They liked the new clothes and the money. The tradition was that you put on your new clothes and knocked on all the street doors.

'My, you look good, so handsome! Turn around for me to see you properly,' the ma would say. Then she would give you some pennies to put in your pocket. Pennies were heavy things and by the end of the tour you were (hopefully) weighed down on one side. Counting them up at the end of the afternoon was the best part. It was even worth wearing the starchy new shirt, the tie, and worst of all, the Brylcreem.

The United Whit Walks were a success, pioneering even. The vicar and Father St John were chuffed to bits as they led them together with the Methodist Minister, all in full robes, smiling.

Perhaps we didn't really understand the significance of this event, at least not at first or indeed for a while to come, but we would reap the benefits of these idealistic young clergy learning their trade with their first parishes and charges.

Across the Irish sea, the Troubles were in full swing. Orange marches and Catholic responses, soldiers murdered and the Bloody Sunday massacre on the Bogside. These Troubles would hit Manchester when, on 4th February 1974, the Provisional IRA would place a bomb in the luggage locker of a coach carrying off-duty British Armed Forces. The bomb exploded between Junctions 26 and 27 of the M6, killing 12 and injuring 38. Peel Hall had its own mix of Protestants and Catholics, and many of the Catholics were originally from Ireland. After all, Manchester was just one stop away from the port of Liverpool. The United Whit Walk was a first step in bringing people together, followed by joint services, Lent study groups, social nights of friendship, all of which played into the birth of stable, respectful relationships between St

Elizabeth's Roman Catholic Church, St Andrew's Methodist and our Church of England parish. Most of all, it created social capital which could be drawn on in difficult times. A model of parish ministry, and Vee and Hal had played their part – a good part.

CHAPTER 12

The 1960s were a decade of huge change and turmoil. Most remember the waves of women's liberation, the 'burn the bra brigade', as Hal would declare them. Music and fashion hurtled from one shocking craze to another. Changes from rock music to mini-skirts, from Mary Quant to Twiggy, the Beatles to the Stones. Tamla Motown became the soundtrack to race riots and the acceptance by some at least that black liberation was not just to be demanded, but needed and deserved. It is no surprise that Vee grew that little bit more confident with the woman she cleaned for – remember the Campari – but even more relevant is that she caught at least a mild spirit of activism. She was beginning to realise that she could make a difference – in fact, she *did* make a difference.

Martin Luther King inspired so many, but for Hal it was Cassius Clay (in 1961 he became Mohammed Ali after his conversion to Islam) who became the hero. The boxing bug had never really left Hal. Although he didn't throw punches in the ring anymore, he still followed it avidly. Clay was a near perfect exemplar who could only be admired. His celebrity proved helpful to a country and a city that was beginning to see growing diversity. Perhaps Moss Side more so, and later – slowly – Wythenshawe, started to see the arrival of immigrants from much more diverse backgrounds, now often referred to as the Windrush Generation. They were treated with some fear and also some real prejudice. They also began, wherever they could, to integrate. Hal was capable of being quite racist. He could make jokes very easily and without any real insight about the impact. Looking back, this seemed terrible but a close look at so-called 'acceptable' TV programmes such as *Love thy Neighbour* reveal the depth of ingrained (and, sadly, accepted) prejudice. At church, one Caribbean family began to settle in and Dolly (the larger-than-life mum of the family) took a shine to Master Harold, as she called him. She and her husband Everett became great friends with Vee and Hal. Despite Hal's blunt talking and clumsy phrases, Dolly adored him. She saw beyond the words and, in her graciousness, she became for him a teacher of how to behave and navigate the world of colour. Most of all, she became a friend. The only white couple at the wedding of their daughter, Hal and Vee were treated like long-lost family members. And that is what they became. Church didn't just blur such cruel boundaries – at best it could destroy them. Hal and Vee learned what the MP Jo Cox would declare many years later: 'There is more that unites us than separates us.' It was a journey for Hal, and for Dolly and her family, but they stepped out together. For Dolly, acceptance by the Millers became a route into their acceptance by and respect of the estate. If Dusty approved, so would many others, whether for good or bad. Fortunately, in this case it was definitely for the good. Hal and Vee were not that aware of their influence. Instead, they followed their gut or intensified intuition: 'contextual intelligence', the academics call it.

There were other darker sides to the 60s' culture. LSD and psychedelic drugs, threats of war such as the Cuban crisis, civil unrest and the disturbing war in Vietnam. The global context and its zeitgeist were never far from the local lives of people. Drugs, as we often hear of them today, were in the main unknown, though the seeds of the future had already been planted. There was always a market on the estate for prescription drugs and the women sometimes experimented with blue hearts, Vee included, but she never really liked them. Hal had his own source of drugs, fully prescribed by the local GP. He took Diazepam and Valium every day to manage the fits, but these drugs were hugely addictive. They provided an easy escape when the going got tough. It was the bane of Vee's life and she was determined to sort it out. Her plan was simple and a little audacious. Basically, she opened some of the yellow capsules, emptied the contents and replaced them with sherbet. She worked on the theory that if she could slowly reduce his intake, things would get better. She didn't plan on getting rid of the tablets altogether. He obviously needed some Diazepam to control the fits, but less was good in her books. It was, and it worked. With a good deal of patience, she improved things, unbeknown to Hal. She was not just a feisty woman, but a wily one too.

The great world event of 1969 was on July 20 when Apollo 11 landed on the moon. The world held its breath as Neil Armstrong walked out of the spaceship, to be joined shortly after by Buzz Aldrin. 'A short step for man and a huge leap for mankind,' he declared. A new era was ushered in, a new future for humanity, a future with no limits. It was, however, a different event that set the estate at Peel Hall alight. That year, the new church of St Richard of Chichester was consecrated. St Richard of Chichester was an unusual choice of patron saint, but if nothing else, gave Peel Hall a distinctive air. Richard was a thirteenth century Bishop of Chichester, a patron saint of farmers. Of course, the whole estate had been built on farming land, so perhaps that influenced the choice. He was a feisty saint who stood up for the poor and was for a while exiled to France, and that too was a useful characteristic to make him appealing to the folk of Peel Hall. Most of all, he was known for his prayer that concludes: 'May we know you more clearly, follow you more nearly, day by day.' That simple emphasis on prayer and taking each day as it comes was also an inspiration for the likes of Vee and Hal.

The new church, described as 'modern minimalist', was designed by architect Gordon Thorne. He often met with the church folk as he worked on the design. It was made of grey brick externally and large greyish stone blocks on the inside. Some say it reflected a monk's cell and was designed for simple prayer and meditation. Its clever use of glazing produced beautiful light which flooded the church, especially on a fine day. Local people also believed the lighting domes in the roof and the lack of windows in the walls were a good antidote to the growing vandalism on the estate. Hal had become church warden earlier that year, and it was to be one of the proudest moments of his life to escort the bishop on the day of the consecration.

Hal had spent many days on the site during the construction. He got to know the lads who worked there.

Making tea on a regular basis, sharing fags, enjoying the craic, it was for him like being at work again and he loved it. The parish took possession of the building properly on the night before the consecration. It was all hands on deck. Vee gathered her friends, the girls from the Brigade, anyone she could accost to join them. She knew that if this was to be our church, the more people involved, the better. Hal and the men from the Men's Society turned out in force along with the lads from the Brigade. The men had made the pews, the women had stitched the kneelers and made the linen. Each group, including the contractors, had bought gifts: elegant cruet sets, a chalice and pattern, vestments and frontals, flower stands and candle holders. They began by scrubbing the floors and polishing the ledges. There was dust everywhere.

The ladies from the Women's Fellowship set to ironing the altar linen and arranging flowers. Joy asked if Vee wanted to join them in the sanctuary, but she said she was better off with her crowd cleaning the floors.

Hal arrived early for the service, ready to meet the Lord Bishop, Dr Greer. He had been preparing what to say and 'Welcome to St Richard's, your grace' was what he settled on. That year he had become the vicar's warden and he'd polished his new churchwarden's wand himself and his colleague's (Brian Simmons's) too. Hal decided this was a teeth occasion – *that* was a mistake. Firstly, nobody recognised him. It looked a bit like Harold, but something was not quite right. Then when he spoke, it was even more of a nightmare. It was hard to understand him as he talked with a whistle and a buzz. (As said before, Vee said he sounded like the radio when you couldn't quite get it tuned in.) The vicar came to the rescue before the bishop arrived. 'Harold,' he said. 'We prefer the old you, the one without the false teeth.' He took them out and wrapped them in his handkerchief with great relief.

What a wonderful day was had by all. The Brigades (lads and girls) paraded the estate, the church was packed full. Geoff served on the altar and managed to carry one of the very heavy marble candleholders without dropping it (and this time without any of the usual bodybuilding wind-up from his tormenting dad). Vee stood proudly with her girls and Gary wore his YBC uniform and joined the ranks of the little Brigade lads. The bishop duly splashed holy water on the four corners of the church, each one bearing a stone from a different cathedral connected to the church; even Chichester had sent one. He then doused the altar with incense (Vee never much liked incense, it was probably her Low Church upbringing, but she put up with it on this day without even a flinch). Hal, with Mr Simmons, processed the bishop in and out with joy and pride; the parish had come of age, too.

CHAPTER 13

There was trouble at Maggie's, big trouble. Trouble at 230 Ashurst Road was not an unusual thing. 'They could argue over the weather,' Hal used to say. This was, however, of a different order; all hell was let loose. Valerie was pregnant. She said she didn't know how, she didn't understand, just that she was sick every morning and her monthly hadn't happened. She came to see Vee, frightened and in tears. Vee tried to talk to her about sex, but she was having none of it – sex, that is. Usually, things were sorted out by shouting or fisticuffs at Maggie's. But no one knew how to handle this one. Hal told Maggie (ordered her even) to get Valerie a doctor's appointment and she did. After the consultation, a termination was agreed as long as Valerie was sterilised, too. Of course, Valerie wasn't consulted; her and the baby's fate was decided by the family and the Social Services. Perhaps it was for the best, but Vee watched this sad girl playing with her dolls, and cried. How it had happened remained, for the time being at least, a mystery. Eventually, after quite a bit of shouting and berating, Valerie admitted it was a boy she had met at the caravan park in Wales. She was in even more trouble and called some pretty awful names. Vee was livid, especially when she looked at the dates which didn't add up – unless she was already 10 months pregnant! She made Hal intervene. 'Tell them to stop it,' she said, 'or Valerie can come and live here. They've said enough, done enough to her, poor kid,'

Hal decided to speak with Valerie. She trusted him more than her own dad. He told her that she was not going to get in any more trouble, but it was best they knew what had really happened. He said she shook with fear. He came home, ashen-faced. 'I think you'd better make that bed up for Valerie. She might need it when I've finished.' Hal went back to Maggie's after tea with a heavy heart, but he had solved the mystery. Valerie had been raped (there is no other word for it) by Bernie's husband. He had sworn Valerie to secrecy on pain of death. She didn't really understand what had happened but Hal was not going to let it go. Houses like Maggie's met such terribly cruel adversity in a variety of ways but mainly kept it within the family. Bernie's husband was dealt with, but not by the authorities. Somehow, they stayed together, perhaps for the kids. It was at least a good thing that his posting to Germany continued for a year or two. Valerie had the termination and the sterilisation; he and Bernie went back to camp. Nothing more was said. More importantly to Vee, Valerie was no longer called the names that should be reserved for idle, ignorant pub talk.

Perhaps it's better that the attention turned to Geoff for a while. Firstly, they noticed a young girl hanging around. A canny little body from around the corner. Time that Hal spoke with his son and gave him the benefit of some fatherly advice.

'Take her to the ice-rink,' Hal advised. 'She'll want to hold your hand so she doesn't fall.' He knew that when they reached sixteen they would be under-age drinking, too. 'Not too much drink,' he said. 'Buy her a Babycham – it comes in a little bottle. If she asks for a brandy to go with it, get rid of her – she'll be too expensive to keep up with.' And that was it! Though he had no real need to worry – they were a sober little couple.

Geoff became more and more involved in the church. In fact, when one of the men dropped out of the retreat at the last minute, Geoff was asked to fill the place. He was barely sixteen, but it would be a good experience. The monks fussed about him and he was mesmerised by the complicated liturgy, the religious bling and the incense. But one thing became clear that weekend at Mirfield: Geoff decided he wanted to become a priest. Hal wasn't sure. Vee thought it was at least possible, but she said, 'Priests don't usually come from our sort.' The vicar was thrilled and the careers' master at school was completely thrown off guard. Nobody from Sharston High went on to college, never mind became a priest! He called him the Bishop of Wythenshawe ever after.

Gary often followed Geoff, but not in this (well, not at this point but later, a lot later, he would shock them). He was more interested in football and horse racing. He put up with school but was looking forward to the day he could leave. He, too, had progressed from thinking that girls made good goalposts when the lads had no jumpers to put down to being a bit sweet on one girl in the Brigade.

What Hal and Vee could feel was that a new era beckoned as the kids started to grow up. They knew they wouldn't have long and they, too, would fly the nest like Brian and Linda. Although Linda, who now had a house in Partington (and an infant son, Karl, to add to the brood), did still come home to visit her mam and dad regularly, with grandkids in tow. Other things on the street were changing fast, too. Flo and Reg had managed to buy their own house on the private estate and had moved there. Jack Waterfield had died of a heart attack just in his fifties. He was the second man in the row to die young, but others would follow. It was par for the course and you didn't need the Black Report on Health in England to back up the figures, though it did. Hal and Vee knew that they couldn't breathe a sigh of relief; they knew that there would be new challenges ahead but nonetheless, life *should* get easier. Hal had a brainwave about money. Inspired by Geoff's desire to buy his own clothes and his hatred at what the clubman could provide, Hal suggested a different plan. They would take it in turns, saving as much as they could, then, in turn, they would have their chance to buy what they wanted with cash. Christmas presents would have to be smaller, but surely that would be better? The four agreed, more than happy with the arrangements. Geoff could shop in town at the trendy shops to buy his looms and tank tops, Gary would just be Gary and let his mum get on with it. Vee could treat herself once in a while and Hal could get his shirts and trousers and make do with the suits he had. It worked a treat, but what was best of all was that Hal could pay off the clubman and the loan shark. For once the Millers would be debt-free – well, almost, because it didn't account for white goods although they didn't have many. At this stage, they had a cooker but no fridge, freezer or washing machine. The only access to HP for large objects was through the electric meter. You had to buy the goods from British Electric, and they did something to your meter so that as well as paying for the electric you paid something towards the cost of the machine. The interest was extortionate and the price of the goods high, but when you had no job, just the benefits, it was the only way to get credit. Vee chose a fridge/freezer first. She was getting sick of 'stera' milk and the butter going off. She said she would go to the launderette now that her very old twin tub had more than packed up. She went on Wednesday nights, under the cover of dark, to Heald Green, a few miles walk away rather than the closer one in the Civic Centre. She didn't know the people there. Geoff went with her. The bulk of the washing fit into her shopping trolley with a full black bag resting on top and Geoff went along to help pull it. He took his school books and did his homework while resting on one of the machines. In a couple of hours, they could have it washed and dried and be back home again. The fridge/freezer was a Godsend, though Hal thought it was more useful than it was. It brought out the meanness in him, especially when Vee caught him trying to freeze lettuce! The kids liked frozen Jubilees in their pyramid cartons and hard cold Milky Ways. Vee was glad just to have fresh milk.

Geoff continued with his idea of entering the priesthood though was dealt a blow when he didn't do so well in his O'Levels. He did, however, go into the sixth form. He was one of just six. He had a couple of teachers who really helped him and he resat enough exams to be able to carry on while at the same time beginning his A'Level courses. Vee was at a loss to help, though she read all the literature text books. She wasn't that fussed on *Memento Mori* by Muriel Spark, found *Jayne*

Eyre okay but long, but she liked *Sons and Lovers* by D H Lawrence. If truth be told, she thought it was a bit risqué for a school book. (It was a good job Geoff didn't introduce her to *Lady Chatterley's Lover* when he 'read around' the subject.) She listened patiently to Geoff's explanation of the Oedipus myth and its application to the book. In this she was a good teacher; she could act daft and he would work harder to explain it all to her. Geoff's pursuit of the ministry never stalled, but he was advised by someone who helped the bishop to do something else first. He applied to a teacher training college near Darlington and was accepted unconditionally – the only one from school to be going off to college! He was set for a new adventure.

Gary, meanwhile, got a job in the office of a freight company. It suited him well and was not far from where his girlfriend, Wendy, would soon be working. He was pleased to be out of the classroom, less pleased that Geoff would soon be leaving. He concentrated on passing his driving test – a real novelty for the family. His first car was a red Mini estate (F Reg, I think). It cost £100, or there about. He thought he was the bee's knees and all the family were thrilled. He would drive to work, take Vee to the shops and the launderette, and drive Wendy around like a real lady.

For Geoff, college opened up a whole new world. The years passed quickly. He would report home to Vee once a week when she called him on the phone. 'You've been on for ages, there can't be that much to talk about. I think you forget about the bill when you get going,' Hal would crib in the background. Vee took no truck with his meanness. She saved what was Geoff's old school bus fare (6d a day) to thwart the running commentary in the background. It was Hal's money, anyway, just reassigned, and in truth, he couldn't wait to get the news too. Fortunately, Geoff got an ample grant. In fact, he had more money than he'd ever had.

Geoff's college experience widened his life in a thousand and one ways. There were new friends from all over the country. He went to visit their homes and, more worryingly, he invited them to his. More decorating and some new towels were needed. Hal was a firm favourite with the college girls and his "sense of humour" made them laugh. Years (many years) later, the family still laughed as they told the story of him watching *The Eurovision Song Contest* with Geoff and a couple of his college friends. Frustrated, Hal declared, 'It's all bloody foreign stuff! They should sing in English at least.'

When Geoff was at home on college vacation, he kept them all entertained with stories of lectures, curriculum classes and the dreaded trials of teaching practices. Vera proved excellent (better than anyone else) at the non-verbal intelligence test he made them all do it as part of an assignment. Perhaps the most memorable event was his graduation after four years. They clubbed together to buy him the Durham hood: 'The only bit of real fur I'll ever have,' Vee cooed when she saw it.

There were only two tickets for the ceremony but Gary, Wendy, Linda and Ash would come anyway. It was to be their first trip to Durham, but not their last. The graduating students robed in their gowns lined up on Palace Green to be processed into the Great Hall of the castle. Geoff, trying to take it all in, heard a whisper, 'Hi Geoff.' It was Aunty Flo with Uncle Reg. Next to them was Dolly from church and Sue Atherton. Then, further along, someone else from the street. 'We got lent a mini-bus from Don at the church so we all came for a day out.' Geoff wasn't sure whether to be proud or embarrassed. That was Ashurst Road for you, and they weren't ready to let him forget where he came from. Life has few enough joys not to share in any that come your way. The college lad was a novelty.

*

Geoff never properly came back to live at home though it always remained "home" to him. He taught in Leeds for a while, but never lost his yearning to be ordained. Hal and Vee always supported Geoff, though they wondered if going into the ministry was a good move. Teaching was for them a well-paid, secure job. He had done well. However, he was dead set and, after a few years teaching, he began training for the ministry. It seemed like almost no time when they were all gathered in Durham Cathedral for his ordination. This time even Brian and his new wife (there's another story there, but that will have to wait for another time) came along. Brian and Ash managed most of the service but after about an hour and a half, they left for the pub. Brian always claimed the pub was full of clergy who had also ducked out early, but that was just his word. The service was solemn and grand, the cathedral full. A coach load of students from the school in Leeds came as well as friends from all over. Another bus load from Manchester and lots of folk from Jarrow, who had already been looking after Hal and Vee when they stayed at Geoff's new home.

Among them was a shy young parishioner and friend of Geoff, Elaine. Little did Vee and Hal know that she would bear them their final grandchild, Philip, albeit sadly too late for them to meet, though at least they did meet Elaine. Linda watched what was happening and was somewhat bemused. 'Why do some of them get to wear lacy white things and others not?' she asked. 'They are the ones not getting married. They are celibate,' she was told by someone who clearly had no real idea. Linda turned to Vee and said, 'They are halibut, them with the lace.' Chuckles went down the pew as the procession began. 'Can you smell fish?' Brian said as they passed. 'Must be the halibut,' retorted Ash.

With that, Geoff was launched into a parish as the new, fresh-faced curate. It was 1984 and working-class discontent was rife; the miners' strike was in full force. Parish life in the North East and the new, fresh-faced curate were in the thick of it. Arthur Scargill was loudly spouting his extreme left-wing diatribes and that "elderly imported American", Ian MacGregor, was calmly organising pit closures and the devastation of communities throughout the north. Behind it was the Iron Lady, the woman who was "not for turning".

It was, however, back home in Manchester where Geoff noticed a real shift, at least in Hal's life. Perhaps it was some residual misogynist tendency triggered by a female Prime Minister; or, more positively, finding again his solidarity with the mining community which he remembered from his youth; or even that Mrs Thatcher evoked a deep matriarchal fear in him. Whatever it was, Harold switched his vote and allegiance to Labour, and did so vocally and enthusiastically.

He had well fulfilled the promise he had made to the local Conservative councillor many years before. Now he had probably found his proper, more authentic voice. Vee had got there long before him, helped by the Campari and the need for a kids' playpark. She had had enough of condescending and uncompassionate folk who thought their money made them a higher order. If she had started out again, I think she would have been a much more vocal activist for her kind of people. She could easily have sorted MacGregor out and sent him packing back to the USA, and she would have given Scargill a run for his money. And, on many occasions, she would have given him a clip round the ear, too!

CHAPTER 14

Next, it was Gary's turn to take the attention. Gary and Wendy, to be precise. They had decided to get married. It was no surprise – they had been together since school days. Wendy's mum had remarried and left the house, so Wendy and Gary could take over the tenancy. Why not then get married? This time, with Geoff, they had their own personal chaplain, so the rest of the plans were made in due course.

It was a wonderful day, the bride glowing and beautiful and Gary sporting a moustache though he had let his Kevin Keegan perm grow out. Afterwards, a crowd of guests escorted the couple to the airport and saw them boarded safely on the plane to Tunisia. I bet they breathed a sigh of relief as they flew off although they would have been a bit embarrassed when the pilot announced his good wishes to them; and I doubt they easily got rid of the confetti strewn through all their clothes as they unpacked later in the hotel.

Though we lived less than a mile from Manchester International Airport, travel abroad was quite a novel experience for all of us. We were more used to clearing the dishes in the departure lounge, sweeping the floors at check-in or, at best, sorting out the luggage. The few girls on the estate who were stewardesses were treated like *Vogue* models in their elegant suits, high heels and their bags on wheels. Of course, for the newly wed Gary and Wendy on honeymoon, this was a recent positive experience, but such examples were few. Hal never went abroad in all his life unless Wales counted. To be honest, he never really wanted to travel, preferring his own bed, his own toilet and his own mug of tea. Vee, however, would have easily got the travel bug. She loved adventure, the new, the exotic, and the faint whiff of luxury. Her first trip to foreign parts was courtesy of her sister, Ethel, who was planning to visit her son Tommy; his latest army posting was in Hong Kong and she wanted Vee to accompany her. It was an opportunity not to be missed and Vee had a wonderful time. Amazed at the temples, the parks and the rich shopping malls, she fell in love with the statues of the chubby sitting Buddha, which reminded her of Hal. (I wonder why?) What she noticed most of all was the plight of the women cleaning and the tired men cycling their rickshaws up hills. In her short time there, she made friends with some of the apartment cleaners, telling them that she did the same back at home in the UK. For quite a while afterwards, to Vee abroad meant Hong Kong and everything was compared with it.

Her second voyage was not a holiday but a pilgrimage to the Holy Land with Geoff and his church. It was a mystical, ethereal time of dreams. Accompanied by Elsie Jefferson from the street and Ethel her sister, the three "girls" had a ball, moving from one encounter to another: The Golden Dome, the Via Dolorosa, the Shepherds' fields, the Bethlehem Grotto and the magnificence of Masada. She was entranced with each wonder paraded before them. But even all that faded into insignificance for Vee as she reached the Galilee. It was for her like heaven on earth. As we took Holy Communion at the lakeside and sang *Dear Lord and Father of Mankind* (especially the third verse), she said it was the most beautiful, peaceful, inspiring experience of her life. 'Bury me here,' she said, and we did – well, we scattered her ashes at least.

The pilgrimage was in 1985 and her third and final trip was in 1988. It was the year of Linda's twenty-fifth wedding anniversary and there was a family party at the Community Centre, the old Civil Defence Centre, to celebrate. The day after, Vee went with Wendy to Benidorm for a week in the sunshine. Quietly, before she left, Vee had confessed that she wasn't feeling that good and was persuaded to see the doctor when she returned. It was to be her last holiday.

I think Hal smelt something was wrong. He hated Vee being away, but he was quiet and patient, and this time he in some ways dreaded her return. This was at the end of August. By Christmas, she was bedridden, waiting to breathe her last. Secondary cancer in the liver! She prepared to die with her usual grace and dignity. Geoff was instructed to contact the brother from whom she was estranged. 'Tell him I want to let bygones be bygones. I want to go peacefully, and I want him to be at peace. No regrets on my part.' He understood and visited. In death, she would also be an inspiration. Her Bingo friends were as kind as all the church ones. The only news that really perked her up was that Wendy was at last expecting. We talked lots over long periods while she lay in bed in that little bunk room (it was the closest to the bathroom).

One night, I asked her, 'Are you not angry with God? Just when things seem stable, even good, then this happens.'

She came back quick as a flash, 'What's the bloody use?'

It was her own home-spun philosophy and she relied on

it. Then she continued,

'It's been a good life in all,' she said. 'I hated the cleaning but got to like the Campari. And I look at you four and the grandkids with some amusement and so much pride. And unlike many people, I've even seen miracles.'

'Miracles? What kind of miracles have you seen?' I asked.

'Oh, real miracles,' she said. 'I've seen betting slips turned into food and debt tabs changed into furniture. You won't beat that.'

We were all watching an old black and white film in her room: *Casablanca*. She remembered the famous lines and smiled as we watched. 'Of all the bars in all the world ...' A few moments later, she stopped breathing. A simple undramatic exit for a woman who had seen plenty of drama.

Hal's world fell apart. This strong, strutting man visibly imploded. Linda tried to chivvy him along. We all did. He stayed with Linda for a few weeks. We thought he was depressed. Well, I suppose he was but that wasn't all. Vee had been his mainstay since he was a young lad. Eventually, he went into hospital with some breathing difficulties, but it was no surprise when the phone rang to call us in and to say that he had died overnight in his sleep. It was just a year since he'd lost Vee and he got his wish to slip away too. He was 63 and Vee had been 61. Both momentous lives, not in traditional terms of success but in how they touched so many others. However, all too short, too short by half.

CHAPTER 15

We started with a question about where and how stories begin or end, and perhaps more to the point if they really *do* begin or end. Our tale has since asked another question, one posed in quiet anger and bewilderment by the stunned young Hal on his wedding day:

'Who the hell is Joe Daniels?'

Hal never got a satisfactory answer to his question. Really, it seems we must reach the end (or at least a pause) without answering either question with any confidence or satisfaction. Perhaps that is just the path of any inquiry and it is foolish to expect anything different. Simple and complete resolution belongs better to the world of novels and Hollywood classics, but this story is about real life. Stories never end in the real world and riddles are rarely solved. Questions usually lead to further questions. Answers never seem complete, never fully satisfy curiosity, rather they often feed it. Perhaps that is their function, perhaps it's the questions that give us the real insight into life. They demand answers, but not ones clothed in finality. Questions instead that open the future.

Since Hal and Ash's research – Hal without much success in the face of Mary Ellen's determined silence, Ash's treks on his moped in an attempt to recover the identity of the Karavitch family and their relationship (or not) with Joe

Daniels – it has become more possible to follow leads. Perhaps a DNA check would be all that is needed to finish the job? But DNA samples of whom?

The progress of the Karavitch family is not difficult to examine, at least from their arrival on these shores. Tailors by trade, a terrible pogrom forced them to leave the slums of the old Russian Empire. Wolfe Karavitch brought his family first to Dublin, then Belfast. Whether they came to labouring posts or to carry on their trade of clothes making, who can tell? They then made their way to Manchester, an international centre at that time for tailors and cloth merchants. With the click of a button, it is all easy to establish. We can find their names, their marriages, the birth dates of their children and their deaths. However, circumstances of all kinds, especially for immigrants and even more for immigrants who are frightened for their safety in the face of persecution, meant that changing and anglicising their names was not an unusual activity. So, somewhere at this point, the inquiry hits a brick wall.

Who is Joe Daniels? Perhaps he didn't really exist, perhaps it was a fake name for a short-lived marriage. Perhaps it was an alias for someone who wanted to keep his identity a secret. But from whom? You could think up so many interesting scenarios but I challenge you to validate any of them. Mary Ellen kept the secret tight within her breast. Searching records seems a futile task. So, there is no answer to offer the reader. Hal lived with this chasm in his identity. It needled him for over 50 years, so what makes you, dear reader, think that you should get an answer? Of course, the story hasn't ended; their deaths just spurred new stories, new lives to open up and live. We can only join Hal, you and I, and ask:

'Who the hell was Joe Daniels?'

ABOUT THE AUTHOR

Geoff Miller is the former Dean of Newcastle. Married to Elaine, he has one son, Philip. He spent 40 years living and working in the North East of England, and is now retired and living in Newcastle. However, he still considers himself a Mancunian and recollects Wythenshawe with some deep affection.

Printed in Great Britain
by Amazon